BEYOND CIVIL RIGHTS:

A New Day of Equality

BEYOND CIVIL RIGHTS

A *New Day* of *Equality*

Hubert H. Humphrey

 RANDOM HOUSE · *New York*

Acknowledgments

I have received much help in the writing of this book, and in the research for it, from William Lee Miller. John Stewart, a member of my staff, provided important materials on civil rights actions in the Senate, and gave the book his continuing attention. Oscar Cohen originally proposed the project, and he and Tedson J. Meyers gave guidance and editorial assistance. I am grateful to all of them, and also to Random House (especially Bertha Krantz, of the editorial staff), for extraordinary work in its behalf.

H.H.H.

To those many Americans who have brought us this far . . . and on whom the new day depends

Contents

A Moment of Truth:
Some Remarks About This Book

This book is an account of American democracy's most difficult test: whether we can achieve real equality for all citizens. I started writing it long before I was a candidate for President, and I did not intend it to be a political document—but now I find that its theme reflects a central issue of a presidential campaign. Will we go ahead to an integrated society, a land of equal rights—or will we turn back? In this campaign of 1968 the American people will make their decision.

This book states what one candidate believes: that the whole modern movement for human rights in America is one continuous struggle—that it is still going on, and that if we are to maintain a free society, it must continue.

Opponents, and some who were once supporters, of this fight for equal rights now disdain it. Many Americans, Negro and white, look upon the movement as finished—maybe even as a failure. Ugly riots, ugly rumors, ugly racisms divide and frighten our people. Burning and looting and white and black terrorism make headlines. But I believe that the human rights movement represents America more truly than any terrorism, extremism, or violence.

Of course, this struggle for equal rights must now change. The older objective (not yet completed, by a long way) was to use the law to strike down racial discrimination. The new objective is to build real equality, especially in the dark ghetto of the American city. This new objective is harder. At the same time (partly because of the success, not the failure, of the older civil rights movement) it has become very much more urgent.

For years I have defended that movement against the right. Now I have to defend it against extremists of both the left and the right. I defend its purpose and method, not because they are "moderate" or "gradual" or a "compromise," not because they represent a "slower" way than some other alternatives—but because they are the only alternative. They are the only way that progress can be made. We must move with the greatest possible speed and energy—forward. My disagreement with extremists is not that they want to go "fast" and I want to go slower—but that I don't think their direction is forward. Grabbing guns, throwing fire bombs, cynically discrediting America's institutions and insisting on racial epithets is not progress —nor will any of this lead to progress.

What we want and must have is equality and reconciliation under the law.

You have to put "equality" first. All of us are deeply concerned now about peace and law, about reconciliation and harmony in America. We yearn to see our country put together again. We want to see all the divided parts of it—and especially black and white— living together in peace. Also, we want to see a revived respect for law and order. We want all Americans to understand, as most Americans do, that there must be obedience to law—even a law that you disagree with—or else we cannot have a civilized society.

But much as we want unity and obedience to law, we do not seek them—we cannot have them—without equal rights. White Americans have to understand that. This is now the precondition of unity and of order.

At the same time, the building of equality must proceed in a way that allows for reconciliation, and that preserves the fabric of law. Any other course will bring neither equality nor order, but chaos, destruction, and new injustices.

Although this book is published in an election year, I hope that it may outlast the particular political season in which it is appearing. The idea was first conceived three years ago, in 1965 (which seems a very long time ago now!), when I was asked to prepare a short book on human rights. The pressure of my duties in Washington delayed its completion until now. If more people read it *because* I am a candidate—so much the better for its objectives.

As I snatched time to work on it, and as the years passed, the nature of the book changed. Originally I had planned a more general and objective treatment, partly a history and partly an argument, which would put before the reading public an overview of the central American subject of equality and human rights. The analogy that was first suggested to me was John F. Kennedy's *A Nation of Immigrants*. As that had presented the story of America and the immigrant, so it was said this could present the story of America and civil rights.

But in the course of actually working on the book it has become more personal. There are two reasons for this change of emphasis.

In the first place, the "Negro revolution" and civil rights obviously encompass an enormous subject—the central feature of our domestic public life, the topic of multiple headlines in daily newspapers and of hundreds upon hundreds of books. I have neither the competence of a scholar nor the time of a professional writer to try to recount the entire history with all its tragedy and heroism—one of the major episodes of American democracy. But though I don't know all of the story, I do know *part* of it at first hand.

It has been my privilege to have been an active participant in the development of major facets of this story for more than a quarter of a century—in the mayor's office of a Northern city; in liberal and civil rights organizations, before civil rights was such a popular topic; in the councils and especially the national conventions of the Democratic Party; in the executive branch of the federal government during the past four years; and, most important of all, throughout the entire modern civil rights movement in the United States Senate. That remarkable institution, for good or ill, has stood at the center of the battle for Negro rights throughout our history. I have been associated with it, as Senator, majority whip, floor leader of the Civil Rights Bill of 1964, and presiding officer, from 1949 until the present moment. At times I was tempted to call this book "The Senate and Civil Rights."

I do not claim that what is written here is the most important part of the whole civil rights story. Who can compare what happens on the buses of Montgomery, Alabama, with what happens in the United States Senate? I have referred in passing to most of the major events of the civil rights movement, but I have told more thoroughly about those that I happen to know about from personal experience.

History did not wait for me to complete this book. As I was finishing it, there was a whole series of major events: entrances, exits, and primaries in the contest for the presidential nominations of both parties; the Report of the Commission on Civil Disorders; President Johnson's extraordinary announcement that he would not be a candidate to succeed himself; the assassination of Martin Luther King, Jr.; riots in many cities, including the nation's capital; the death of Senator Robert Kennedy; and my own nomination for the Presidency.

So now the book must bear a larger meaning than originally intended, for a pervading issue in the presidential election of 1968, as in this book, is the relation of the races in our society—the relation of justice to law in America.

The most dangerous third-party candidate for President in this century owes his political existence exclusively to the fears and hates aroused by that issue. And decisions taken this past summer suggest that the Republican candidate may contend that ground with the independent candidate.

By a curious historical development, I now find myself facing two opponents, both of whom have the approval of my long-time extreme antagonist in the civil rights battle, J. Strom Thurmond. In 1948 Mr. Thurmond led the segregationist walkout after the Democratic Convention adopted a strong civil rights plank, and ran as the Dixiecrat candidate for President against Harry Truman. In 1957, when all the other Southern Senators decided not to filibuster against the compromise civil rights bill, Thurmond alone conducted a one-day one-man attempt to kill it. In the 1960's—now a Republican—he has consistently been the most extreme spokesman against the great civil rights acts. I am proud to have been his chief opponent on these matters consistently throughout twenty years no matter what party he belonged to.

And now here I am opposing a Republican presidential candidate who was escorted to the podium, to make his acceptance speech, by J. Strom Thurmond, and who planned his strategy for the nomination and cleared his choice for Vice-President with Thurmond.

For about a quarter of a century now our country has been making steady progress toward equal treatment under law: an FEPC; the desegregation of the armed services; the adoption of a strong civil rights plank at the 1948 Democratic Convention; the Truman civil rights program; the 1954 Supreme Court decision, outlawing legal segregation; the Montgomery bus boycott; the 1957 and 1960 Civil Rights Acts; the sit-in movements; the freedom rides; the voters' education projects; the comprehensive 1964 Civil Rights Act; the Voting Rights Act of 1965; the Civil Rights Act of 1968. We have turned the country around, from a time when law and government *supported* segregation and discrimination to a time when law and government *oppose* segregation and discrimination.

And as a result of all this, there have been civil rights activities by many institutions beyond the federal government: local and state government, business, labor, the churches, schools, universities.

Looked at in the perspective of history and considering the perennial problems of divergent groups living together, this quarter century of American progress has been one of mankind's great stories.

It has been too slow. It came very late. But it *did* come. It came in a *lawful* way. And the pace has been accelerating.

Until now we have been moving steadily forward, making progress under law, together, Republicans and Democrats, black and white, the North united with a growing part of the South.

Hitherto, as the reader will see from this book, the civil rights movement has been bipartisan. But now in 1968 there comes a crossroads: a dangerous election, a hazardous national choice.

Are we going to move backward into separation and fear, into a society in which the races live in hostile enclaves, in which every man is continually conscious of his race, in which no man is safe from a mindless violence that may strike him solely because of his color? (And I mean no man in the suburbs as well as in the cities; in the North as well as in the South.) Are the dire predictions of the white and black extremists to be proved true?

Look at the seething cauldron of the cities, listen to the talk of white vigilantes and of black revolutionaries, watch the sale of guns and the making of firebombs, look at the flight of white people and the mounting anger of black people—is that the way America ends, after all the dreams that mankind had for this nation?

Does the land of the free and the home of the brave turn into an armed camp?

What will our choice be—apartheid or democracy? Separation or community? A society of ordered liberty or a society of fear and repression?

I believe American citizens do not want to live in a land where every man fears his neighbor.

This nation has a moderate majority, black and white, in the North and in the South. That vast preponderance of the people believe neither in racism and repression, nor in revolution and riot.

They want to extend equal treatment to every man— and they want to do it through the law.

I believe that this moderate majority will prevail.

But whether it prevails or not, this is where I stand. My record on this issue includes the proudest moments of my public career. I would not deny that record, or change it, or tone it down, even if I could. And I want it to be said, then, of Hubert Humphrey: He stood by what he believed.

Hubert H. Humphrey
Waverly, Minnesota
September 6, 1968

1

"The Bright Sunshine of Human Rights"

I would like to think that upholders of the progressive-populist-liberal-reformist tradition, which is my own heritage in American politics, had steadily fought against complacency and racism through all these years. But it isn't true: for one long and important period they deserted the Negro. Although the Populist movement, for example, was interracial in its early days, by the 1890's it began to develop a strong racist strain. In fact, in the early years of this century some of the worst demagogues came from a Populist background.

The political psychology is worth noting, because we are not free of it even today. Believing in equality and the common man, the movement ran up against the difficult fact that many "common men" who were white had prejudices against the Negro. Also, the social condition of the subordinated Negro reinforced prejudices. That created grave difficulties for a theory of equality, and many people held on to this theory by limiting it to whites—by racism.

The Progressive movement of the early part of this century was not aggressively racist, but neither did it have racial equality as a central plank. The expression of progressivism in my own party was often represented by a Southern gentry that was not egalitarian on race. Woodrow Wilson, a hero of mine, is, I am sorry to say, an example. During his administration segregation was instituted in federal government office buildings.

It was not until Franklin Roosevelt became President that the condition of the Negro became an important issue in the main work of American liberalism. And it was not until the Democratic Convention of 1948 that racial equality was firmly endorsed by a major American political party.

When Franklin and Eleanor Roosevelt came to the White House (and it is appropriate to name the First Lady as well as the President), there began to be a change. "In the thirties," wrote Arthur Schlesinger, Jr., "Franklin Roosevelt gave the Negroes a sense of national recognition. He did so more in terms of their interests in economic and social justice than of their title to equal rights. Yet he threw open the gate of hope . . ." Although the New Deal did not face up squarely to the issue of equal rights, its social and economic programs were of benefit to the Negro, who has always been the "last hired, first fired" in the American economy. Negroes in great numbers switched from the Republican to the Democratic Party. The New Deal also made the Democratic Party unequivocally the party of progressives and reformers.

And yet it was not until the years after World War II that we really began to break down the segregation system.

The Pattern of Jim Crow and Lynch Law

Some Americans today may have forgotten what that system meant. It was worse even than the discrimination other groups faced—bad as that often was. The Irish faced the indignity of signs that said "No Irish need apply"; the Italian found that he was not accepted in the social club; the Jew faced anti-Semitism in many forms. But the Negro alone has faced a whole structure of exclusion *by law*, not only from residential areas and social clubs, but from schools, theaters, restaurants, railroad cars, political party primary elections, and from a whole host of public and private facilities: the Jim Crow pattern of segregation.

Many Americans do not realize that this was a *new* pattern, not at all derived from slavery. It was deliberately invented and imposed long after the Civil War and a considerable time after Reconstruction, for the most part in the 1890's.

Professor C. Vann Woodward of Yale quotes an editorial *against* segregation in railroad cars which appeared in a conservative Charleston, South Carolina, newspaper as late as 1898:

"As we have got on fairly well for a third of a century, including a long period of reconstruction, without such a measure," wrote the editor, "we can probably get on as well hereafter without it, and certainly so extreme a measure should not be adopted and enforced without added and urgent cause." He then called attention to what he considered the absurd consequences to which such a law might lead once the principle of the thing were conceded. "If there must be Jim Crow cars on the railroads, there should be Jim Crow cars on the street railways. Also on all passenger boats . . . If there are to be Jim Crow cars, moreover, there should be Jim Crow waiting saloons at all stations, and Jim Crow eating houses . . . There should be Jim Crow sections of the jury box, and a separate Jim Crow dock and witness stand in every court—and a Jim Crow Bible for colored witnesses to kiss. It would be advisable also to have a Jim Crow section in county auditors' and treasurers' offices for the accommodation of colored taxpayers. The two races are dreadfully mixed in these offices for weeks every year, especially about Christmas . . . There should be a Jim Crow department for making returns and paying for the privileges and blessings of citizenship. Perhaps, the best plan would be, after all, to take the short cut to the general end . . . by establishing two or three Jim Crow counties at once, and turning them over to our colored citizens for their special and exclusive accommodation. . . ."

The editor was intending with heavy irony to reduce the whole idea to absurdity. And yet, as Mr. Woodward points out, in a very short time the irony turned around:

Apart from the Jim Crow counties and the Jim Crow witness stand, all the improbable applications of the principle suggested by the editor in derision had been put into practice—down to and including the Jim Crow Bible.

In his excellent book *Alarms and Hopes,* Senator Fred Harris of Oklahoma gives the following detailed description of segregation:

Negroes were prohibited from using the same public accommodations or conveyances, and the law enforced separate or segregated schools and hospitals, prisons, restaurants and bars, hotels and boarding houses, toilets, railway and streetcars and waiting rooms. Negroes and whites could not use the same water fountains or ticket windows. They could not mix in fraternal societies or at circuses, parks, race tracks and sports events. They could not live in the same residential areas, nor could they even be buried in the same cemeteries . . .

New Orleans required separate districts for its Negro and white prostitutes. Oklahoma required telephone companies to provide separate telephone booths for Negroes and whites. White and Negro school textbooks had to be kept and stored separately in North Carolina and Florida, and the mixing of the races while playing dominoes or checkers was specifically prohibited in Birmingham.

In a touching line in a Langston Hughes' poem, a little Negro girl asks: "Where's the Jim Crow car on this merry-go-round?"

All this was done *by law*.

Again and again in the arguments over civil rights laws we proponents used to have to refute the constant plaint: "You cannot change men's hearts by laws." There are many good answers to this familiar American mistake:

The first is that the primary intent of these laws is to make real the rights of the black man, not to alter the psychology of the white man; another is that the point is not to change white men's hearts but to change their behavior (otherwise you could make the same objection to every law, from that against murder to traffic regulations); yet another answer is that you *can* change hearts, in the long run, by using the law to change experiences: segregation bred prejudice; and integration, as the generations advance, can help to overcome it.

And there is still another point to consider: law created the evil pattern of Jim Crow in the first place; law therefore can help to overcome it.

The real point of segregation was not separation but subjugation: the system was intended to humiliate the Negro and deprive him of power. The separate schools, hospitals, and public facilities provided for Negroes were almost always obviously and grossly inferior to those provided for whites. The real point, in the prejudiced white man's psychology and power system, was not so much to keep the Negro separated as to keep the Negro *down*. There was no strong objection to sheer *contact* with Negroes—after all, they had been nursemaids, mammies, house and body servants, mistresses. The objection, rather, was to Negro *equality*, to his being "uppity" and "not knowing his place" (just think about what those once-widespread phrases really mean).

Again and again the truth would slip through in argument with segregationists. I remember a moment in the Senate, during the filibuster against the 1964 law when there was only a handful of us on the floor, and the Southern Senator whose turn it was slipped away from the strictly constitutional and legal arguments that ordinarily were used and began to explain to us in a friendly, reasonable way—as one white man to other white men, so to speak—that what really worried his fellow white citizens in the South was that they would be overwhelmed by the mass of Negroes, and that was why they prevented Negroes from voting.

"Just how do you square that with the Constitution?" I asked him quietly. At which point other filibustering Senators hastened into the chamber to get the subject back to the abstract and impersonal constitutional grounds on which they were trying to argue.

Segregation, therefore, was a system of group *power,* of *subordination*—of inequality. And one more ugly fact has to be mentioned: it was maintained, to a shocking degree, by violence. The period around the turn of the century that saw the reimposition of subjugation on the American Negro was also the period that saw a great increase in lynchings. The white-mob lynching of Negroes became almost an institution, tolerated, if not actively encouraged, by many respectable white leaders. The tradition of condoning violence against Negroes (and "nigger-lovers" among the whites) continues down to the civil rights struggles of our own day; we are just now moving into an era when a white man can be found guilty by a Southern court for violence done to a Negro or civil rights worker.

The Effect of World War II

The resistance to this segregation-subordination system was gathering force in the New Deal days. Then the coming of the international struggle with Nazi Germany accelerated it. It is sad and ironic that it needed to be so, and yet it was—fighting demonic racism abroad, the American nation became more embarrassed by its own racism at home.

The generation of World War II was the first in which great numbers of white Americans learned that racial equality is the most important of all the issues in American democracy. That realization was coming anyway, but it was greatly hastened by the encounter with a racist enemy abroad. Thus the war with fascism educated some white Americans.

But it was especially painful to Negro Americans. And James Baldwin wrote about what it meant to be a black American soldier in World War II:

> You must put yourself in the skin of a man who is wearing the uniform of his country, is a candidate for death in its defense, and who is called a "nigger" by his comrades-in-arms and his officers; who is almost always given the hardest, ugliest, most menial work to do; who knows that the white G.I. has informed the Europeans that he is subhuman (so much for the American male's sexual security); who does not dance at the U.S.O. the night white soldiers dance there, and does not drink in the same bars white soldiers drink in; and who watches German prisoners of war being treated by Americans with more human dignity than he has ever received at their hands. And who, at the same time, as a human being, is far freer in a strange land than he has ever been at home. HOME! The very word begins to have a despairing and diabolical ring. You must consider what happens to this citizen, after all he has endured, when he returns—home; search, in his shoes, for a job, for a place to live; ride, in his skin, on segregated buses; see, with his eyes, the signs saying "White" and "Colored," and especially the signs that say "White Ladies" and "Colored Women"; look into the eyes of his wife; look into the eyes of his son; listen, with his ears, to political speeches, North and South; imagine yourself being told to "Wait." And all this is happening in the richest and freest country in the world, and in the middle of the twentieth century.

The Negro soldier came "home," and so did the white soldier, and America has not been the same since. In the AVC and ADA, in the student movements and in the churches, and in the hearts of many Americans there was a determination that segregation must go.

Harry Truman became President just as the war was ending, and he offered the first comprehensive presidential program for civil rights in our history. In early 1947 he appointed a civil rights committee; in October of that year the committee issued a historic report called "To Secure These Rights." That report proposed a national FEPC, an anti-lynch law, a civil rights commission, protection for the right to vote, statehood for Alaska and Hawaii, home rule for the District of Columbia, and other measures—a program we have been working on ever since. In February, 1948, President Truman sent a civil rights message to Congress, proposing legislation based on that committee report.

This civil rights program reflected a widespread moral conviction in postwar America. Many items in it could command the support of a majority of the people and of Congress. But the filibuster in the Senate blocked its enactment.

There was one thing Mr. Truman could do without congressional action: end one of the most disgraceful of America's racial disgraces—Jim Crow in its fighting forces. This he did. Though there was initial resistance in the Navy and other armed services, they have now (perhaps a little ironically) become one of the most fully integrated of American institutions.

The first postwar and post-Roosevelt national convention of the Democratic Party became, then, a historic occasion. The Democratic Party was the party that had equivocated on slavery in the 1850's, the party of the South, the party that had not supported the civil rights acts after the Civil War—but it was also the party of Thomas Jefferson and Andrew Jackson, the party of equality, reform, and the common man, the party of Franklin Roosevelt and of Harry Truman's civil rights proposals. There was a great moral backlog of issues postponed by the war. Where would the party stand on human rights in 1948? In the national convention of that year the long battle for equal rights at last became the basis of the program of one of the great national political parties.

The writer of this book had the good fortune to be a participant in that event. The party's new position might soon have been adopted anyway. If I had not been the spokesman for it, someone else would have been; but I happened to be the one.

A Mayor's Role and a City's Responsibility

I grew up in the little town of Doland, South Dakota. Doland was so different from Harlem that a television producer once devised a program contrasting my boyhood with that of James Baldwin—complete opposites, it was implied. And we were a long way from the problems of the city and the ghetto out there in that Midwestern town. But we did know about the problems of the countryside, including the poverty of the depression years. I remember my father crying when he had to sell our house. I myself had to leave college to help support the family during that dark time.

I was raised as a liberal and a Democrat by my father, who was a wonderful, humane man, truly a remarkable man, a kind of small-town philosopher and natural democrat. When as a young man I entered politics, it was as a reformer and a progressive, along the lines that my dad had taught me. He used to read to me from Thomas Jefferson and William Jennings Bryan and Woodrow Wilson. One of the main ideas I learned from him was that of human equality, which encompassed—in the perhaps rather dated words people used back then—"tolerance" and brotherhood."

Doland was rather a homogeneous and parochial Midwestern Protestant town. There weren't any Negroes there. But Doland was nevertheless more or less egalitarian in spirit, and it was explicitly so in my father's drugstore. One man was as good as another—that was what democracy was all about. My father's vote was one of a grand total of five for Al Smith in the entire county in 1928 (he was the Democratic county chairman in that election).

My mother, who was more conventional than my father, used to get a little uneasy because I had some friends she thought were too unusual, but my father encouraged us to know and understand all kinds of people. Shantytown in Doland was where poor kids lived, and I had friends there, though my mother frowned on some of them.

Once there was a big road-construction job on the edge of town; a lot of the workmen were Negroes. I used to sell newspapers to the townspeople and also to these workmen, and pretty soon they let me ride the mule teams with them and sit beside them on the steam shovel. When they'd come into town, people would stare at them—most of the folks had rarely seen a black man. But the men would call me by name as they went by, and I'd get up on the wagon seat with them. This horrified my mother, but my father was pleased.

Years later, and long after I left Doland, I made my first trip South to go to graduate school in Louisiana. I was greatly shocked by my first encounter with racial segregation.

I was shocked again a few years later, when I ran for Mayor of Minneapolis and discovered for myself the heavy weight of bias in that Northern city, too.

I lost on my first try for the mayor's office in 1943, but then in 1945 I won. My campaign theme, second only to an attack on rackets and corruption, was human rights.

It may be a little hard for a person now living in Minneapolis to believe, but that city was then a center of bigotry, with an evil pattern of anti-Semitism. It was so bad that a Jew could not even join the Automobile Association. When I became Mayor I suspended a couple of policemen who had made anti-Semitic remarks. The small number of Negroes were ignored altogether in the city's life.

In my campaign I often quoted Carey McWilliams' statement from the early 1940's that Minneapolis had become "the capital of anti-Semitism." When I got to be Mayor, I instituted a number of reforms that, I think, are still relevant today, more than twenty years later. One had to do with the police. Though Minneapolis' Mayor does not have much formal power, he does appoint the police chief. I appointed a new one, an excellent man and by chance a neighbor of mine named Ed Ryan. I had a long fight to get him approved by a citizens' group—which is another story. After he was in we worked out a "human relations" program for the police—the first, so far as I know, in the country. We sent the police to school to study human relations at the Center for Continuation Studies at the University of Minnesota.

I appointed a Mayor's Council on Human Relations, headed by Reverend Reuben Youngdahl, pastor of a large Lutheran church, whose brother was the Republican Governor of the state. I asked many community leaders to help me in an "education campaign" on human rights in Minneapolis. My idea was to appeal not only to the citizen's sense of injustice but also to his sense of civic pride. We should be ashamed, I kept saying, of "this evil, decaying thing in our community." I initiated a "community self-survey" in which citizens, with the help of professional interviewers, made studies of areas of discrimination and tension in Minneapolis. (Walter White, then head of the NAACP, was one of those who helped us with this survey.) And we found, for example, that some hospitals would allow only Caucasian doctors to practice.

This community self-survey and the education campaign—through speeches and the work of the Mayor's Council—were, in part, a preparation for a more difficult task, the enactment of a municipal Fair Employment Practice ordinance. Our strategy was first to make the citizens realize—by the means I have mentioned—just how bad discrimination in Minneapolis actually was (as in most cities, the citizens do not face the facts and admit the way things are until you force them to), and then to enact into law an instrument of changing it. We succeeded enough to win an award from the National Conference of Christians and Jews as the "Brotherhood City" in my last year as Mayor.

Citizens of Minneapolis came to be soberly aware of the discrimination in their city, but it was still very difficult to get the conservative City Council to enact an ordinance setting up a fair employment practices commission (FEPC). The Mayor in Minneapolis, under a non-partisan "weak Mayor" system, had little formal power; the twenty-four-member City Council was strong, quite conservative, and reluctant to set up any FEPC with real power. Therefore, we had to build a fire, lit by the public, under the City Council. The situation was not unlike the one that prevailed in the Senate and in the country during the years leading up to the Civil Rights Acts of 1964 and 1965: There was very broad support for civil rights among prominent and responsible citizens, but still much resistance in the populace and among legislators who have to face the voters. It is a continuing situation that always requires a most careful and thorough political strategy—to translate broad moral conviction in the community into votes in legislature, overcoming the partly hidden resistance of inertia, conservatism, fear of change, racial fears, racial prejudice.

In Minneapolis we did that by a year and a half's campaign, first rousing the city's conscience by the means I have mentioned, and then lobbying for months with individual city councilmen. As Mayor, I talked with every councilman, and the eminent local citizens on the Mayor's Council on Human Relations kept appealing to the councilmen, too, and lending their prestige to the campaign. Finally, in January, 1947, we were successful: Minneapolis' City Council enacted a strong Fair Employment Practice ordinance. The text was written for us by a young lawyer named Orville Freeman. It was the first municipal FEPC in the nation.

The March on Washington

More recent civil rights activists may not know what those initials signified, politically and morally, back then. They stood for the most advanced and important —and controversial—of our postwar civil rights proposals. They symbolized all that was to follow.

The "FEPC" had acquired, by January, 1947, a considerable history. Back in early 1941—with the war already raging in Europe and with defense production rapidly rising in this country—there was a confrontation with President Roosevelt about the employment of Negroes in military production under government contract. American Negroes and American liberals were not going to stand for the prevailing inequality and discrimination. They were not going to accept racism at home in the very industries that were making weapons to fight racism abroad.

If you look back at those days you will see how bad the situation was. For example, the head of one great aircraft corporation, which then and today, under contract with the United States government, employs thousands of Americans, made this flat statement in the spring of 1941: "Regardless of their training as aircraft workers, we will not employ Negroes . . . It is against company policy."

The general organizer of a large union said: "Organized labor has been called upon to make many sacrifices for defense and has made them gladly; but this [admission of Negroes to the union] is asking too much."

These were not isolated examples, but all too representative. The state employment services cooperated with employers who discriminated, and even federal defense training programs practiced racial bias. In the early years of the war in Europe the employment of American Negroes actually worsened.

Against that background, Negro leaders planned the first famous March on Washington, which they intended to hold on July 1, 1941. The chief leader of this effort was A. Philip Randolph, the founder of the Brotherhood of Sleeping Car Porters and one of the greatest of living Americans. A broad cross section of the Negro community participated. The number of marchers anticipated was first estimated at 10,000; then 50,000; then 100,000. President Roosevelt and administration leaders pleaded, negotiated, made offers. But the offers were inadequate and were rejected. Finally, on June 25, the President agreed to what the marchers wanted—an executive order banning racial discrimination in defense plants. The march was called off, and Roosevelt issued the famous Executive Order 8802, establishing the wartime FEPC.

That march (or proposed march) was more successful than some other, later, demonstrations, in part for these reasons: the objective was limited, specific, uncomplicated, and unarguably just, and it was entirely within the power of the executive to grant it.

This wartime FEPC, of course, had many enemies in

Congress, within the administration, and among the public. Nevertheless it was a success. The opponents who argued that it would not work were proved wrong. And a great many of us were convinced that a permanent national FEPC should be a top priority after the war.

New York set up the first state FEPC in 1945, and many other states followed; Minneapolis set up the first municipal FEPC in January, 1947, and other cities followed; and meanwhile many of us hoped for and supported a national FEPC. President Truman's committee recommended it.

A key point, of course, was the need for *enforcement* power. In some situations an agency which can only conciliate, persuade, and publicize may still be better than nothing; in other situations it may be a fraud and therefore worse than nothing. But the best FEPC would have real powers. Conciliation and persuasion are *very* important in this whole field, and we should rely on them to the fullest possible extent. In the federal efforts now, more than twenty years after the events I have been describing, we use such voluntary means to great effect in activities like "Plans for Progress," a cooperative business-government program for equal opportunity. But the methods of concilation and persuasion are effective only where you have one or other of these: a strongly supportive public opinion (which we have in Plans for Progress) or strong enforcement powers (which we had in Minneapolis, and which we wanted in a federal bill). In Minneapolis our ordinance was tough. It provided jail terms and fines for violations, and set up a commission to administer the law.

Enforcement provisions are needed, not necessarily because they are going to be used very often—one hopes they won't—but because they make the efforts at persuasion effective and they put the force of the law on the side of the man who wants to do right (instead of leaving him alone and exposed.)

In Minneapolis we demonstrated another feature of such strong anti-discrimination laws: they have an effect beyond the specific cases that they touch. The structure of discrimination crumbled rapidly in Minneapolis after we passed that ordinance, without the necessity of taking many cases to court. The city's two biggest department stores, for example, began to hire Negro clerks.

Many states and cities have since passed an FEPC law. When did we get a *federal* law? Not until the Civil Rights Act of 1964.

Meanwhile the FEPC had become, through the wartime experience and after, a powerful symbol for the opponents of civil rights, as well as for the liberals. It was a red flag to the segregationists. Of course, there were many other civil rights issues, but FEPC symbolized the crucial point to both sides: the purposeful, active use of the law to break down racial discrimination.

The Convention of 1948

I think that was what was really at stake in the famous floor fight at the Democratic Convention in 1948. If you read our "strong" platform plank now, twenty years later, it may not sound like much, but it did call on Congress to support the President in guaranteeing fundamental rights like "the right to equal opportunity of employment." That means an FEPC.

The situation in that Democratic Convention was as follows. We met in Philadelphia in a hot July of 1948 (in an auditorium with no air conditioning) to nominate the incumbent Democratic President, Harry Truman, who was widely expected, even privately by Democrats, to lose. Our battle over the civil rights plank—the only real fight at the convention—was made more difficult because of this doubt about Mr. Truman's chances in November. Much of the resistance to our support for a strong plank was put in these terms: what you are doing will split the party, lose the South, and insure the election of the Republicans.

I went to the convention not only as Mayor of Minneapolis but also as a Democratic candidate for the Senate in the fall election (Minnesota had never elected a Democratic Senator). I was chairman of the Minnesota delegation, and a member of the 119-man platform committee.

I went also as one of the founders of a new liberal anti-Communist organization, the ADA, which we had started the year before. The ADA was important in the events that followed.

The first shots in the civil rights battle had already been fired, long before I actually arrived in Philadelphia. There had been strong representations from liberal forces such as the ADA who wanted a plank that meant something. We wanted a platform stand that went beyond the vague statements of 1944 and earlier, and that pledged the party to support Truman civil rights measures, including an FEPC.

In the fight for such a pledge we had to make not just one but two hard decisions. The first was to oppose the subcommitee that presented a weak plank to the platform committee. The second came when we had lost in the platform committee, and decided to carry our fight to the convention floor.

The first battle took place on the weekend before the convention and continued on Monday and Tuesday, the convention's first days, behind closed doors. It was long, and it was heated in more ways than one. Inside those closed meetings of the platform committee Andrew Beimiller, then a Wisconsin Congressman, and I fought and fought for a stronger civil rights plank. It was hot; the fight was long; and some tempers were lost. The elders of the party were all against us, arguing monotonously that we were going to split the party and elect the Republicans. They said we would cause a Southern walkout. They said we were defying the wishes of the President. They said the 1944 platform of FDR should be good enough for all Democrats. At one point Scott Lucas of Illinois, who was the Democratic leader of the Senate, pointed at me and called me a "pipsqueak." He said I wanted to redo Franklin D. Roosevelt's work and deny the wishes of the present President of the United States.

I called a meeting of the Minnesota delegation, to consult with them, and they urged me to continue the fight for a strong plank. Late in the day on Tuesday, however, after we had met all day, the platform committee voted down the strong plank by about seventy to thirty.

Then I had to face the second decision. The arguments of the party elders did bother me, especially after we were defeated in the platform committee. The issue then was whether to take our minority report to the floor of the convention itself. I was, after all, a young and very junior member of the party. I was thirty-seven years old. We were opposed by all of the party hierarchy: the President (so we were told); National Party Chairman McGrath; Convention Chairman Rayburn; Senate Democratic Leader Lucas; the platform committee chairman, Senator Francis Myers of Pennsylvania; and many others.

My own father, who was chairman of the South Dakota delegation, had a sober talk with me about my responsibilities to the party. At first he, too, was rather against what I was considering doing. I remember it very well. It was in my room on the fourth floor of the Bellevue-Stratford Hotel. Finally my dad said: "This may tear the party apart, but if you feel strongly, then you've got to go with it. You can't run away from your conscience, son. You've got to go with it."

The decision to take the minority report to the convention floor was much harder to make than the earlier decision. After all, we were told, you had your say in the platform committee, and you lost, so now you should close ranks and support the committee. The events on the convention floor, unlike those inside the platform committee, would be open to the public (not yet by television, but by radio and the press), so that to take the issue to the convention floor would be to take it before the entire nation. It would expose our party differences. It would offend the South. And—

everybody said—we couldn't possibly win. Even the ADA proponents never thought we could actually carry the convention. The party big wigs all said: Don't try. Most of the press called us "kids," and said we had no chance.

But Andy Beimiller and Joe Rauh and other young leaders of the ADA were determined to take the issue to the floor. The ADA had its own informal headquarters at a fraternity house of the University of Pennsylvania, and in that headquarters the line was clear. And they wanted me to be the spokesman. We met at the frat house, and we had an all-night meeting about it in my hotel room (no suite in those days; refreshments were on ice in my bathtub). I was bothered by the arguments against making a floor fight; I didn't want to split the party or to damage President Truman's chances. (Other people were telling me I would ruin my own political future if I defied the party leadership in this war. After all, it was a fruitless cause, and I was running for the Senate. When I got to the Senate the next year there *were* many Senators who held this action against me). Finally, at almost five in the morning, we worked out a formula that convinced me. We would propose a strong plank, but we would introduce it with solid praise for Mr. Truman's civil rights program.

We had less than ten hours before the fight on the floor that Wednesday afternoon. I worked on my speech; the others tried to line up support among the delegations. Andy Beimiller called Speaker Rayburn, the convention chairman, and told him we were going to offer a minority report on civil rights. Rayburn said the Southerners were going to offer one, too—in the opposite direction. He explained that he thought the defeat of the Southerners' plank would balance off ours, and bring victory to the "moderate" administration plank.

That afternoon—like all the others—was hotter than a pistol. As I was waiting to make my speech I still had uneasy feelings. Sitting on the convention platform, with my speech in my hand and a big yellow Truman button on my suit, I mentioned my doubts to my neighbor, a party stalwart, and he encouraged me to go ahead. Readers who remember that period will be surprised to learn who this was. It was not one of the established liberals of the party—but Ed Flynn, the "boss" of the Bronx.

I was more than a little scared that afternoon—I don't want to pretend I was a paragon of virtue. I didn't want to split the party, and I didn't want to ruin my own chances in politics—which were the two arguments people kept making to me. I was a young fellow, and this was my first real experience at a big convention. Before this I had only heard of Ed Flynn, and there I was sitting beside him. I started to show him what we were proposing, in an apologetic way.

"Look," I said. "Here's what we're asking. It isn't too much. We think we ought to make the fight. I'm sure we don't really have much chance to carry it, but we ought to make the fight." And I said: "We surely would welcome your advice."

He looked at what we were proposing and he looked at me—I'll never forget it—and he said: "You're damned right. You go ahead, young man. We should have done this a long time ago. This is long overdue. We've got to do it. You go ahead. We'll back you."

I said: "Will we get any votes?"

He said: "You'll get votes."

"Will we get New York?"

"You'll get New York."

"Will we get Pennsylvania?"

"You'll get Pennsylvania and you'll get Illinois."

I said that Francis Myers of Pennsylvania, chairman of the platform committee, was opposing us.

"He'll change," said Flynn.

I pointed out that the Senate's Democratic leader, Scott Lucas of Illinois, had been very strong against us.

"You'll get Illinois," said Ed Flynn.

He said he would talk to Jake Arvey of Illinois and David Lawrence of Pennsylvania—two more "bosses" to the newspapers and bad guys to us in the ADA—and he did. Flynn was really solid. So was David Lawrence. After Flynn talked to him, Lawrence came over to me and said: "We'll back you. Pennsylvania will back you."

And then Arvey came up and said: "We'll back you."

So when I got up to give the speech I knew we weren't as far behind as we'd thought the night before.

Andy Beimiller read the minority plank that we proposed, and then I gave my speech— my first to any such important gathering. It was carried by radio across the country. Even though I still feared we would lose, I felt that the speech was reaching the heart of the Democratic Party.

First I paused and looked out over that big audience.

Then I began in what I hoped was a conciliatory way (I was trying to do then what I would try to do sixteen years later, when the same emotion-charged conflict finally came to the Senate floor: keep it as restrained and free from personalities as it could be).

I realize I am dealing with a charged issue—with an issue which has been confused by emotionalism on all sides. I realize there are those here—friends and colleagues of mine, many of them—who feel as deeply as I do about this issue and who are yet in complete disagreement with me.

My respect and admiration for these men and their views was great when I came here.

It is now far greater because of the sincerity, the courtesy, and the forthrightness with which they have argued in their discussions..

Because of this respect—because of my profound belief that we have a challenging task—because good conscience demands it—I feel I must rise at this time to support this report . . .

Then I tried to make clear that the strong plank was not aimed just at the South.

All regions and all states have shared in the precious heritage of American freedom. All states and all regions have at least some infringements of that freedom . . .

I knew very well, from my experiences in Minneapolis, that that was true.

Then I tied my thought to the heart of the party by referring to the well-liked Vice-President-to-be, who had also been the convention's keynote speaker—and through him to Thomas Jefferson.

The masterly statement of our keynote speaker, the distinguished United States Senator from Kentucky, Alben

Barkley, made that point with great force. Speaking of the
founder of our party, Thomas Jefferson, he said: "He did
not proclaim that all white, or black, or red, or yellow, men
are equal; that all Christian or Jewish men are equal; that
all Protestant or Catholic men are equal; that all rich or
poor men are equal; that all good or bad men are equal.
What he declared was that all men are equal . . ."

We are here as Democrats. But more important, as Americans— And I firmly believe that as men concerned with
our country's future we must specify in our platform the
guarantee which I have mentioned [*i.e.*, the guarantee of
equal participation in the blessings of free government].

Then I set this in the international scene. It was the
practice in those postwar, early cold-war years to make
these international comparisons.

Our demands for democratic practices in other countries
will be no more effective than the guarantees of those practices in our own country.

There are those who say to you: We are rushing this issue
of civil rights. I say we are a hundred and seventy-two
years late.

All my life I have been arguing with people who say
we are moving "too fast" even when we aren't moving
at all.

There are those who say: This issue of civil rights is an
infringement on States' rights. The time has arrived for
the Democratic Party to get out of the shadow of States'
rights and walk forthrightly into the bright sunshine of
human rights . . .

This turned out to be the emotional high point of
the speech.

Let us forget the evil passions, the blindness of the past. In these times of world crisis we cannot—we must not—turn from the path so plainly before us.

For all of us here, for the millions who have sent us, for the whole human family—our land is now, more than ever, the last best hope on earth.

I know that we can—I know that we shall—begin here the fuller and richer realization of that hope, that promise of a land where all men are free and equal . . .

I occasionally hear it said that I talk too long—but that Philadelphia speech was short, lasting less than ten minutes. It created a response in the convention hall that went far beyond my dreams and hopes. The Minnesota delegation leaped to their feet (they were surrounded by Southern delegations). California, down front, stood and cheered. Soon there was a great demonstration—a most vivid memory to me—a demonstration unlike the manufactured ones for candidates, because it was really spontaneous and it reflected a deeply felt endorsement of a principle. Of course, it was not the speech that led to the demonstration, but a great ground swell in the Democratic Party and in the people—a ground swell of conviction that had at last found an outlet in the major politics of the nation.

The state that led the demonstration was—Illinois, Scotts Lucas' home state. The man who picked up the Illinois banner and first started around the hall was a Chicago alderman and economics professor who was soon to be a Senator—Paul Douglas. I can still see him, with his great head of white hair, carrying the Illinois banner, leading that tremendous demonstration. (That fall Paul and I were both elected to the Senate. Sixteen

years later, when we finally enacted the Civil Rights
Act of 1964, I was sitting in the front row of the
Senate chamber, as floor leader of the bill, and Paul
was sitting a couple of rows directly behind me. When
they announced the vote I looked around and caught
Paul's eye. We finally did it.

Two years after that, in the 1966 elections, after
three remarkable terms in the Senate, Paul was defeated. He came out flatly for open housing and refused
to hedge or trim, despite what everyone [and the polls]
said the opinion was among white working-class districts, normally Democratic, around Chicago. He went
down to defeat as bravely and honorably as he won his
victories and served justice in the Senate.)

But to return to 1948 in Philadelphia—it was a memorable demonstration. California followed Illinois, and
many other Northern and Western states fell into line.
We wanted the band to play, but Speaker Rayburn
gaveled it down. He pounded for order, but the demonstration went on for eight minutes. After it subsided,
there was a new spirit in the hall.

The delegates then voted on the States' rights minority proposal, and easily defeated it. Then the roll was
called on the Humphrey-Beimiller strong plank. The
vote was close, and the lead went back and forth. The
states of most of the national leaders went against us,
but we got a great deal more support than we had
dreamed possible. Hubert Humphrey, Sr., cast South
Dakota's eight votes—"Aye!"—for our plank. When
it came down to Beimiller's Wisconsin delegation, we
were moving into the lead—and Wisconsin voted
twenty-four votes "Aye." I knew then we had won,

and jumped to my feet. The auditorium filled with loud applause and cheers.

When the vote was announced, it established that indeed we had won—651½ votes to 582½.

A group of young liberals had beat the whole leadership of the party. The ADA forces carried me—literally—back to the fraternity house, and we had quite a memorable celebration.

But far more important than the victory and the glee of our small group was the deep current in the party and in the country that made it possible. We were the reflection of what a great company of Americans felt and believed in the years after the war.

One can explain the victory in that convention—in part—in realistic political terms. Ed Flynn and David Lawrence and Jack Arvey and John Bailey of Connecticut probably supported us—in part—because they wanted a winning issue in a difficult year. Maybe they wanted something to attract the votes of liberals, Negroes, minorities, and labor, and to protect against the appeal of Henry Wallace's Progressive Party on the left. Also, perhaps there were those in the Northern urban wing of the party who didn't mind offending the South, since parts of the South had deserted Al Smith back in 1928. But those realistic—or cynical—explanations take us only a short way. All my life I've heard our civil rights proposals derided, by conservative columnists and white-supremacy orators, as merely efforts to win "the Negro vote" (in Minnesota? I feel like saying). I think the cynics tell more about themselves—the narrowness of their outlook—than about the real world. There was a lot more to that vote in

Philadelphia than practical politics. Along with their practical sense those organization leaders do have their convictions.

David Lawrence, for example, showed it all his life. He was an interesting man, a true politician and a man of idealism. I later came to know him well. In the Kennedy administration, years later, he was the head of the President's Committee on Equal Housing. He kept struggling to keep this committee an active force during the administrations of both Kennedy and Johnson. I can remember his pleading with me to get more done for open housing than was effected by President Kennedy's very limited executive order. The fair housing provision finally enacted in the Civil Rights Act of 1968 is in no small measure the result of the work of David Lawrence.

All across the hall in Philadelphia that afternoon in 1948 there were people like Lawrence who would later be heard from on the subject of equal rights. Many were voting *against* the "realistic" advice of the hierarchy—because of their convictions. I think of my father and those South Dakota votes, and Andy Beimiller and those Wisconsin votes, and, of course, our delegation from Minnesota—and a great many more like that. It was a great moment. The Democratic Party had made a new commitment.

When the result was announced, delegates from Mississippi, Alabama, and a few other Southern states stood up as though to leave—but Speaker Rayburn quickly declared the meeting recessed. When we reassembled two hours later to vote for the presidential nominee, thirty-five Southern delegates, led by Governor J. Strom Thurmond of South Carolina, walked out of the hall into the rainstorm outside. In November the Dixiecrat Party gave Thurmond thirty-eight Deep South electoral votes.

But Harry Truman won the election.

2

"The Old Universal Urge
Toward Freedom"

From our earliest days there were Americans who opposed slavery—Quakers, humanitarians, religious leaders. In the 1830's the movement for the abolition of slavery became the most important expression of America's social idealism.

Many Americans, then and later, disapproved strongly of the abolitionists, and didn't want to be associated with them. Many American historians have looked on them with disdain—as unrealistic and emotional radicals who, although they fought for a moral issue, were not responsible or intelligent in the way they agitated for it. But historian Richard Hofstader, discussing one of the most outstanding abolitionists, Wendell Phillips, made this observation:

> Historians in condemning men like Phillips have used a double standard of political morality. Scholars know that the processes of politics normally involve exaggerating, mythmaking, and fierce animosities. In the pursuit of their ends the abolitionists were hardly more guilty of these things than the more conventional politicians were in theirs. Somehow the same historians who have been indulgent with men who exaggerated because they wanted to be elected have been extremely severe with men who exaggerated because they wanted to free the slaves.

Some history books serve up the Civil War simply as a matter of sectional and economic forces, to which the issue of slavery was quite subordinate. Yet if you study the best of the reformers, you can see that there was also a strong American social idealism that repudiated slavery on moral grounds. This was true of the leading literary intellectuals—among them, Emerson, Thoreau, and Channing—and it was true of a prophetic minority of the clergy, who were the chief leaders of the early wave of abolitionism—men whose names most Americans don't know, such as Theodore Weld.

There were many black leaders, including such instigators of slave revolts as Nat Turner, who has been brought to public attention by William Styron's novel. (It shows how selective is our teaching of history that this event has been otherwise so little known.) There were articulate ex-slave leaders of abolition, the most famous of whom was Frederick Douglass. There is a whole Negro history that the nation is just beginning to learn. There were many whites who served in the underground railroad that aided escaping slaves. There were a million readers of the sentimental but effective *Uncle Tom's Cabin*. There was enough anguish over the evil of slavery to make the nation's moral logjam a major reason why we had a bloody Civil War.

Light at the Low Point

The nation did not follow through in a humane and realistic way after the war, with educational and economic programs to help the ex-slave become a full citizen. It did not even protect his rights. But in the darkest days of the late nineteenth and early twentieth centuries there were still some spokesmen for racial equality. W.E.B. Du Bois, the distinguished scholar and writer, presented a more penetrating and prophetic outlook than did Booker T. Washington, whose strategically accommodating philosophy was more acceptable to the white man's ears. Some of the themes of the long debate between Du Bois and Washington are still relevant today. The Kerner Report links current black separatism to Booker T. Washington's outlook. Du Bois, who advocated many differing philosophies throughout his long life, was in the earlier days an uncompromising champion of integration, equality, full civil rights, full Negro franchise, higher education for able Negroes; he refused to accept the racial subordination and separation that much of the white world believed that Booker Washington accepted.

There were white spokesmen for equality even in the worst days of the turn of the century. In 1908, after a bloody riot in Lincoln's hometown of Springfield, Illinois—whites attacking Negroes—a group of white humanitarians led by Mary Ovington and Oswald Garrison Villard sent out a call for a meeting and a new organization. They combined forces with a group of Negro intellectuals formed a little earlier under Du Bois' leadership at Niagara Falls (on the Canadian side, because facilities on the American side were segregated). Out of this combination there came a new organization that has ever since been at the center of the battle: the National Association for the Advancement of Colored People.

In those days it was the radical group, taking a militant stand against Booker T. Washington's accommodation to the white world; some people today, sixty years later, see the NAACP as having switched over to the moderate or conservative side, standing against the new militants. But it has not changed; it has steadily worked across all these years for equality and integration under the law.

It is curious how these labels shift around: "moderate," "militant," "conservative," "liberal." The Urban League, also founded early in this century, has often been regarded as the most conservative or moderate of all the organizations in this field. Yet the excellent work the Urban League does, especially in operating with business and finding employment for Negroes coming into a city, is now again right on the cutting edge of the most up-to-date approach to these problems. Lots of times these labels don't make sense. One must look behind them to see what is really happening. And when one looks, one sees, for example, that the Urban League under Whitney Young is carrying out effective programs in city after city.

Through the bad days of World War I (with a Jim Crow army) and the worse days after that war—when many cities had bloody white riots, and when the Ku Klux Klan revived in power not only in the South but in the North the NAACP and the Urban League worked steadily year after year to protect and enlarge the rights of the black American, and to improve his life.

The NAACP's main emphasis has been the law. As early as 1915 the organization began winning the cases in the courts that would build toward the decision of 1954—which, in turn, ushered in the modern period of intensive action for Negro rights. The NAACP has been at the forefront, also, in lobbying for new legislation for civil rights—for all the laws we have passed—at the state and local levels as well as in Washington. It had provided legal assistance to Negroes throughout the years, and has fought a steadily broadening battle to recover the Negro's right to vote.

Du Bois, James Weldon Johnson, my friend Walter White, Roy Wilkins, one of the wisest of American leaders, Clarence Mitchell, who has led a thousand fights in Washington, Justice Thurgood Marshall, the martyred Medgar Evers, Aaron Henry, and hundreds of others—all great names in Negro history—have been active in the NAACP.

The NAACP has been interracial from its inception, although the major part of its membership has been black. I have been proud to be a member for many years. I hope the day never again comes in America when an organization is looked down on for having an interracial membership.

Once during World War I, when the organization was looked on as "radical" and was protesting the treatment of the Negro soldier, agents from the Department of Justice visited its headquarters and asked Dr. Du Bois "just what is this organization fighting for?" Dr. Du Bois replied: "We are fighting for the enforcement of the Constitution of the United States."

That's what the NAACP has done for six decades.

Civil Rights in the Mainstream

But the prophetic minority did not reach the conscience of the larger American public until after World

War II. Since then the civil rights movement has brought into play, one after the other, the nation's major institutions and groups.

President Truman made his path-breaking proposals in 1947. The Democratic Party made its new commitment in 1948. The first step with major practical consequences was taken not by Congress (to which Mr. Truman's proposals and our platform plank were addressed) but by the United States Supreme Court. *Brown v. Board of Education*—the school segregation cases—of 1954, and other decisions, struck down the legal basis for racial segregation.

The next major step was that of demonstrations and direct action by masses of committed citizens, beginning with the remarkable Montgomery bus boycott of 1955. Direct action took other forms, later, in student sit-ins and the freedom rides of 1960 and 1961; the Washington March of August, 1963; the "Mississippi Summer Project" of 1964; the Selma March of 1965, and in many lesser demonstrations.

Meanwhile, influenced by the direct-action movement and by changing opinion, the other two branches of the federal government had begun to play a major role.

The Presidency assumed a central place on the night of June 11, 1963, when President John F. Kennedy came before the American people and made his historic speech after the disorders in Birmingham. He placed the full authority of his office behind the moral requirement of equal treatment, and he called for a comprehensive civil rights act, which was to become one of his chief memorials. Lyndon Johnson, immediately upon becoming President, increased the presidential pressure for that civil rights act. He led the struggle for Negro rights through his strong support of the Voting Rights Act of 1965, and by his great speech at Howard University; he sponsored the White House Conference in June of 1966, and backed the national fair-housing law that he has signed into law as I write these words.

The Court and the Schools

The decision of the United States Supreme Court in the school segregation cases of May 17, 1954, was one of the great moments of our time and one of the profound turning points of American history. But it was not as sudden or as unexpected as some citizens seem to think, nor as much a reversal of what had gone before.

The Court did reverse the doctrine of "separate but equal" that had been upheld in the case called *Plessy v. Ferguson* in 1896, but that case had itself been a reversal of the meaning of the Civil War constitutional amendments. *Plessy v. Ferguson* held that public facilities could constitutionally be "separate but equal", but the facilities—schools for example—were very far from being "equal."

The Supreme Court cases in the field of higher education, beginning in 1938, challenged the notion of "separate but equal." The Court said then that for Missouri to pay a Negro's expenses to go elsewhere, out of the state, to do graduate work did not meet the test of equal treatment. In 1950 the Court said that a Texas effort to set up an "equal" law school for Negroes could not succeed: the intangible elements in the process of learning the law would never be equal in the separated schools.

So the doctrine of "separate but equal" was already punctured when the school segregation cases began to work their way up to the Supreme Court—from Kansas, South Carolina, and elsewhere—in the early 1950's. On May 17, 1954, the great decision was handed down, saying that "segregated schools are inherently unequal." It was really no surprise, and certainly no violation of American precedent. On the contrary—it was a reaffirmation of what this nation has always claimed to be. It was also in line with a steady development of the earlier cases. It was the *Plessy v. Ferguson* 1896 doctrine of "separate but equal" that was out of step with American democracy.

The Truman administration, in its last days, submitted an important brief supporting the plaintiffs. This brief called the "separate but equal" doctrine "an unwarranted departure, based on dubious assumptions of fact combined with a disregard for the basic purposes of the Fourteenth Amendment, from the fundamental principle that all Americans, whatever their race or color, stand equal and alike before the law." That is the real American precedent.

In 1955, a year after the first Brown decision, the Supreme Court decreed that implementation must be accomplished "with all deliberate speed." The first reaction to the decision among segregationists had been rather mild and resigned: they would, after all, have to obey the law. In border states and the District of Columbia many school districts were soon integrated. But gradually opposition mounted and hardened.

Many commentators have said this happened partly because there was not a clear-cut indication from the President that the decision was morally right and that as the law of the land it must be obeyed and would be enforced.

Some eminent Southern leaders openly began to counsel defiance. The Senate soon became the center of a hardening Southern resistance. Eminently respectable colleagues in the Senate drew up a "manifesto" attacking the Supreme Court and its Brown decision, and almost every Senator from a "Confederate" state felt he had to sign it (Lyndon Johnson of Texas, then the majority leader, and the two Senators from Tennessee—Estes Kefauver and Albert Gore—were the only ones from the old South who did not sign). Senator Harry Byrd of Virginia, a very powerful and respected leader not only of the government of his own state but of the whole South, set out a course of "massive resistance" that encouraged an attitude of defiance in many areas.

In retrospect we can see that the period between the Supreme Court's decision of May, 1954, and the Little Rock crisis of September, 1957, should have been a time for strong initiative by the federal government to underline the necessity for obedience to law and the firm commitment by the executive to enforce it. But it was not. In February of 1956 the federal government allowed the Governor and other officials of Alabama effectively to defy a federal court order admitting Miss Autherine Lucy to the state university. The early handling of the defiance at Little Rock reflected the same pattern. There was no firm federal action to indicate unequivocally to all concerned that court orders must be obeyed and that federal law would be enforced. The sending then of federal troops, when the defiance continued, came as a sudden large jump in policy—from persuasion to paratroops—by the federal government. President Kennedy, in the 1962 struggle over the admission of James Meredith to the University of Mississippi, tried to avoid the pattern of Little Rock. He was firm from the start, and yet held off using federal troops.

The old segregation *by law* has slowly diminished. At the same time, de facto segregation, in the cities of the North as well as the South, has increased.

As Bayard Rustin, the distinguished long-time leader for social justice, has pointed out, a Negro parent who saw his child enter a segregated first grade in 1954—when the Supreme Court handed down its decision—probably saw him graduate in 1966, still from a segregated school. After the 1954 and 1955 decisions we kept trying to enact legislation that would allow the Federal Department of Justice to intervene in ways to accelerate desegregation, but we did not succeed until 1964. The desegregating of public schools remains the most difficult area in which to make meaningful advances.

We have made many small gains. Under new court orders and new Health, Education and Welfare guidelines we will now make further and much larger advances. But the history of the effort to desegregate the schools demonstrates how interrelated all the parts of the fortress of racial inequality really are. It shows that we must attack simultaneously from all sides and in the context of a larger social and economic program.

Because the Court started this modern sequence with the public schools in 1954, and because those schools are under the control of a public agency, we have put very heavy pressure on the schools to desegregate, and in some cities to seek "racial balance."

Until very recently we have not accompanied those actions with comparable efforts in other fields.

Housing patterns, especially as between the city and the suburb, have become *more* segregated.

The difference between suburban and inner-city schools has been gigantic—as measured in per-pupil dollars and other indices of educational quality. (Private schools, of course, have always been available to the well-to-do.)

Our equal-employment efforts and hard-core job programs have just begun to go beyond tokenism.

But now, in the late sixties, we are attempting to put together some of the laws and tools for what we need: a balanced, many-sided attack on racial inequality in a setting of social programs for all the poor, and of economic progress for all Americans.

The favorable economic setting is essential, so that jobs and houses and better schooling for Negroes do not appear to be a direct threat to the hard-won advantages of blue-collar or white-collar whites. A broad social program is necessary for that reason, too, among others.

The desegregating of the schools, for example, should be accompanied by open occupancy in housing, a good education for all Americans, and new educational monies for the hard-pressed inner-city schools.

In order to overcome racial inequalities, there must be social change. Both justice and prudence indicate that that change should come as reform on a wide front rather than attempted revolution in one sector.

Racial "imbalance" is not the only kind of imbalance in our schools. The mammoth imbalance in resources between the richest school districts and the poorest school districts calls into question our adherence to our own American democratic ideas: the universal free public school system. Thomas Jefferson believed an educated citizenry was the essential foundation of democracy. Americans have, presumably, always subscribed to that idea, and it lies behind our public school system. Yet the disparity among districts and among schools in real educational quality is so great as to raise a question about our basic belief in it. And it will take more than racial integration of schools to solve this problem.

Direct Action

The Court made its school decision in 1954 and 1955. Then in 1955 and 1956 another actor stepped onto the stage: the ordinary Negro citizen.

Although for many years individual Negroes of exceptional advantage or exceptional bravery had found ways to participate in the fight for equality, the mass of poor Negroes had not. These very inequalities—

lack of power, disenfranchisement, lack of money, lack of education, isolation from the main institutions, plus all the ugly white brutality and intimidation—had long kept the black masses relatively passive. This passivity allowed some complacent whites to rationalize racial injustice by saying, "Well, they are happy as things are!"

One great result of the Montgomery bus boycott of 1955 was the destruction forever of that idea; since that event no American can soothe his conscience with the foolish notion that the Negro is content. And the mass of black Americans found in that boycott a way for them to participate. It is one thing to hear about the Supreme Court decisions and votes in the Senate; it is quite another to take a hand yourself, and by direct participation to affect your own destiny.

After discouragement and retrenchment in the late fifties, another kind of direct participation in 1960 touched the nation's conscience and started a more intense period of civil rights activity: Negro students in Greensboro, North Carolina, staged a "sit-in." That type of protest spread rapidly and caught immediate public attention. Other forms of direct action, demonstration, and peaceful protest followed, especially including the "freedom rides" through Southern states in 1961.

None of this was new, but the public attention was new. I have described the first march (or almost march) on Washington led by A. Philip Randolph back in 1941. Although it was successful and a remarkable event (Randolph called the resulting Executive Order 8802 a "second emancipation proclamation"), and although the Negro press featured the story, the general press ignored it entirely or played it down. Most Americans in the summer of 1941 knew nothing about any "March on Washington."

After the war there were a number of protests and demonstrations, including sit-ins and picketing, but the public was not watching them. As a freshman Senator in 1949, I joined in a demonstration against the National Theater, a segregated theater in downtown Washington—which most of my colleagues regarded as quite un-senatorial behavior.

The organization called CORE is not a product of events in the sixties or even the fifties, as some now think, but started as an outgrowth of a pacifist organization, the Fellowship of Reconciliation, back in 1942. Even then it was developing and using nonviolent techniques such as the sit-in and the freedom ride. When at last these orderly civil rights demonstrations came to public attention in the sixties, they already had a long history of practice, development, and discipline.

A Virginia newspaper (*Richmond News Leader*) published the following about a sit-in in Richmond on February 22, 1960 (the kind of comment that could not be made about many subsequent protests):

Many a Virginian must have felt a tinge of wry regret at the state of things as they are, in reading of Saturday's "sitdowns" by Negro students in Richmond stores. Here were the colored students, in coats, white shirts, ties, and one of them was reading Goethe and one was taking notes from a biology text. And here, on the sidewalk outside, was a gang of white boys come to heckle, a ragtail rabble, slack-jawed, black-jacketed, grinning fit to kill, and some of them, God save the mark, were waving the proud and honored flag of the Southern States in the last war fought by gentlemen. Eheu! It gives one pause.

In the sixties this movement grew into the remarkable March on Washington in August, 1963, which helped to pass the Civil Rights Act of 1964, and the Selma March of 1965, which helped to pass the Voting Rights Act of 1965. These peaceful demonstrations caught the nation's attention and aroused its conscience, helped to pass these great legislation enactments, and helped to regenerate America's social idealism after the doldrums of the fifties. They gave the ordinary Negro citizen a way to participate in shaping his own destiny, and a way for idealistic young white Americans to express their devotion to social justice. They were most effective where they stayed within the law; had a specific objective; violated no one's liberties; and where the participants were the victims rather than the perpetrators of the resort to force. The nation owes a great debt to the hundreds of brave Americans—like Mrs. Parks on the Montgomery bus and the students in Greensboro—who participated in this extraordinary movement. They represented and helped to revive the humane purpose of American democracy.

Think, for example, of the Negro youngsters in the first days of school desegregation (and some still today) walking bravely past mobs of hissing adults. Here is what novelist Ralph Ellison said once back in 1961:

You know, the skins of those thin-legged little girls who faced the mob in Little Rock marked them as Negro but the spirit which directed their feet is the old universal urge toward freedom. For better or worse, whatever there is of value in Negro life is an American heritage and as such it must be preserved.

There is a worthy white section of that American heritage, too, alongside all the ugliness. As Protestants, Catholics, and Jews marched together down an Alabama road in 1965, an angry white citizen on the sidelines challenged a nun: "What are you trying to do to the white race?" he asked. "Educate it," she replied.

That is the real American tradition—the one we want to preserve and enlarge—of people who were not only repelled by the institutions of racial subordination but who worked bravely to overthrow them.

3

The Senate
and the Filibuster

When I came to Washington in 1949 as a freshmen Senator, it was a segregated Southern city, and the Senate was the institution in which the South had its greatest power. Seniority is very important in the Senate, and so are committees; both of those facts increased the power of the South. In that solid one-party region, nomination as a Democrat had been equivalent to election. Once elected, a Southern Senator could ordinarily count on continued re-election, building up his seniority while competitive two-party states would be defeating incumbents and electing freshmen—like Paul Douglas and me in 1949— who would be starting at the bottom of the ladder. Committee chairmanships and committee assignments were given strictly on the basis of seniority, and the committees and chairmen have very great power in the Senate. The chairman of the Senate Judiciary Committee could block those civil rights bills that we introduced merely by refusing to hold hearings on them or to report them to the floor. Each year at Christmas time I worked privately on committee assignments with Lyndon Johnson after he had become Senate Democratic leader. Once he said to me that it would take eight years to get a judiciary committee that would report civil rights bills.

The Southerners were the patriarchs of the Senate. Many of them, like Senators George and Russell of Georgia, were very able and honorable men who carried great weight with the whole Senate, not only because they had seniority and held powerful chairmanships, but also because they had knowledge derived from many years of experience and were respected for their character and ability. It was very hard to go against them in the United States Senate of those years.

The atmosphere of the Senate was courtly, gentlemanly, leisurely in pace, full of tradition and propriety —and sometimes racially discriminatory. It is a little hard to believe now, with the interracial staffs all over Capitol Hill, but when I hired a Negro in 1949 he was one of the first on a Senator's staff. He was Cyril King, then a graduate student and now Lieutenant Governor of the Virgin Islands. One day I took him with me to the Senate dining room. As I came in the maître d', an older man and a Negro who was a dear friend of mine named Paul Johnson, took me aside (I was a brand-new Senator) and said, with great embarrassment: "Senator, I don't know quite how to say this to you, but— but the Senators don't bring colored men into the Senate dining room, and I think it may cause you a considerable amount of trouble." He was so embarrassed he could hardly speak. He was a dear good man, and he was trying to protect me, I suppose. He had taken a liking to me and I loved him. But I wasn't very tactful to him. I said with some asperity: "Mr. King is a friend and he's my guest and I don't give a damn whether they like it or not. He has been in my home. Anyone who is good enough to come to my home is good enough for this ptomaine parlor.'' And we ate there, and I later took Mr. King again and also George Weaver and other Negroes, and I never heard anything about it from anyone.

I did hear what some of the older and more conservative Senators thought of me, though. After that speech at the convention of 1948 and the Southern walkout I was a marked man.

In the first sessions in which I served, I introduced legislation

— to establish a commission on civil rights,
— to set up a federal FEPC,
— to outlaw the poll tax in national elections,
— to provide equal access to public interstate travel
— to protect rights guaranteed by the Constitution and federal law,
—to protect the right of political participation.

I joined in sponsoring anti-lynching bills.

Did we have a chance of passing any of these? Not much, not then. But we were building toward the day when there would be a chance. Most of them are now law. I have kept a list of the measures that I introduced in those early sessions, in this field as in others; most are now checked off.

But back in 1949 and in the early fifties my continual introduction of such bills just confirmed the negative impression of me held by many conservative Senators after the 1948 convention.

As a result of my activities at that convention, many old-time party leaders looked at me with aversion when I showed up on their own home ground, the Senate, in the following January. One day in the cloakroom I overheard an older Senator say to another: "What in the world do the people of Minnesota mean, sending a damn fool like that up here?" The conservative newspapers—and they were a large part of the press then—kept writing about me as though I were the wildest radical who ever came out of the woodwork. And I made some mistakes myself that didn't help matters. For example, one day I rather brashly attacked the favorite committee of the revered Senator Harry Byrd, and I did it when he wasn't on the floor—which is against the proprieties—and, as I didn't know, when he was absent because of an illness in his family. The next day Senators on both sides of the aisle really unloaded on me. They even turned their backs on me on the Senate floor. Those first years as a Senator were unshirted hell for the ex-Mayor of Minneapolis and ex-hero (or villain) of the 1948 convention.

Gradually, though, things changed. I began to dine in the Senators' private dining room with some of the Southerners, and although they had to put up with my convictions, they found I wasn't so bad personally, and I grew to like and admire many of them. In my 1954 race for re-election the esteemed Senator George of Georgia wrote a kind letter for me which startled some of my Minnesota supporters and my ADA friends.

During the 1952–54 period I came to know and work with another Senator who had much better connections than I did at that time with the congressional powers, the inner Senate club, and the Southerners: the new Senate Democratic leader, Lyndon Johnson of Texas.

I discovered that he was a lot more liberal than many thought he was. I could work with him and he could work with me. He taught me a lot about how to get things done in the Senate, and I think I had an influence on his social outlook. We worked together, and I became more acceptable to the Senate and more effective.

But that didn't pass any of the pocketful of civil rights bills I would introduce at the start of each session. I chaired the first Senate hearings on a fair employment proposal, hoping that would influence someone, but it didn't. I cut back to a minimal proposal, a Civil Rights Commission to make investigations and reports. I sent letters to editors across the country, urging this as a first step; the conservative editors attacked the proposal as dangerous and radical, and the handful of liberal editors attacked it as a sell-out. We didn't get very far in the early fifties.

Relations within the Democratic Party improved somewhat, though. At the 1952 convention a stronger civil rights plank than that of 1948 was adopted, with an anti-filibuster item for the first time—and there was no Southern walkout. An able moderate Southern Senator, John Sparkman of Alabama, was the vice-presidential nominee on the ticket with Adlai Stevenson.

But the 1954 Supreme Court decision on school desegregation changed that and hardened the lines of division. I have mentioned the Southern "manifesto," and the way honored Senators gave respectability to the defiance of law. On the whole, those were difficult years for civil rights in the Senate.

In the late forties and in the early and middle fifties the civil rights forces in the Senate were a very small band—twenty-five votes at most, and we could not always count on all of them. For the most part we lacked seniority. At first we had few important committee posts. There was a deliberate effort by the dominant conservative powers in the Senate to divide and weaken us. Herbert Lehman of New York, Paul Douglas of Illinois, and I kept introducing civil rights bills and fighting for them, but we didn't get anywhere until 1957. The years before that were only a preparation.

The 1958 election, plus our growing seniority, changed the complexion of the Senate, and we liberals were no longer an embattled minority. From that day to this we have been able to win some victories in the Senate.

The Filibuster

But we have always faced the barrier of the filibuster.

You have to understand the Senate, and you also have to know something about the American history on civil rights to realize how important the filibuster has been.

From 1875 until 1957 –through almost a century of war and peace, depression and prosperity, lynchings and hardening Jim Crow laws, vast migrations and social changes—there had been no federal legislation whatever for the civil rights of Negroes.

The guarantees of these rights enacted after the Civil War had later been stripped away, and nothing had been put in their place. Actually, around the turn of the century, the plight of the Negro had been made even worse. There had been no new federal civil rights legislation through all this period even though, in the later years (the years since World War II), a majority in both houses of Congress would often have supported such legislation. Why couldn't we enact it? Because of the filibuster in the Senate. And because the commitment of the public was not great enough to overcome it.

The jealously guarded Senate tradition of "unlimited debate" had sometimes served the common good—but it has also given an enormous negative power to a small section of the nation and a small minority of Senators. It has meant that the eighteen or twenty Senators from nine or ten states again and again could kill any civil rights bill just by talking it to death.

The filibuster (or threat of a filibuster) time and again prevented us in the Senate from even considering the civil rights bills that liberal Senators like myself would keep introducing, that the House of Representatives (where there is no filibuster) often would pass, and that a majority of the Senate would have favored if they had been allowed to vote.

Were it not for the filibuster we could probably have had for some years now a federal FEPC and maybe even some kind of an open-housing law; we could certainly have had much earlier and stronger protection of voting rights, and federal intervention to aid school desegregation. The filibuster has given a recalcitrant minority excessive power, and made the legislation we *have* passed come later and in weaker form than it would otherwise have been.

Therefore, along with our efforts to pass civil rights bills we also fought and fought against the filibuster. We kept trying to mitigate the closure rule to limit debate—usually to make it possible to close debate by a majority vote instead of two-thirds.

I do not mean to say that the recurrent fight over the filibuster is entirely a reflection of convictions on civil rights, There was also, mixed into it, a powerful tradition about the value of unlimited debate in the Senate.

And virtually all Senators share that tradition. I have spent most of my adult life in the Senate; as I write this I am the President of the Senate. I fully appreciate the great merits in our system of government of this extraordinary deliberative body. I know from experience the merit of the tradition of full and unhurried debate, in which public questions may be examined with a thoroughness not possible elsewhere in government.

An independent Senate is a valuable part of our system of government. It provides a chance for a second look, and is an essential check on the President and the executive branch. Citizens who don't like the Senate's independence on one issue find that they do like it in another.

And, of course, by no means all filibusters have had to do with civil rights. In my youth there were filibusters by the progressive Midwestern Republican Senators. Later, during the Kennedy administration, a group of liberal Senators, led by Wayne Morse, Estes Kefauver, and Albert Gore, staged an unsuccessful filibuster against the Communication Satellite bill. Still later Paul Douglas himself led an "extended discussion" for forty-four days against Senator Dirksen's bill to delay reapportionment. (That last instance is the clearest modern example of the positive value extended debate can have: Senator Douglas and his colleagues gradually educated the Senate and the public, changed the minds of some who listened, and in the end brought significant softening of the measure.)

But I believe that all the merits of the Senate's tradition of full debate can be preserved without giving in to the disgrace of minority rule by lung power. Full debate, yes; talking endlessly just to kill a bill, no.

I would like to see a more reasonable Rule XXII (the two-thirds closure rule). As it now is it not only violates the spirit of majority rule; it violates the spirit of the Constitution. Wherever the Constitution requires a two-thirds vote, it expressly says so; elsewhere, the majority rules. I think it should be possible to close debate in the Senate by a majority vote; the commitment to full debate is deep and strong enough to protect against abuse, in my opinion.

Beginning in 1949, when Paul Douglas and I first came to the Senate, there has been a fight over this matter at the start of almost every session. They have all been complicated. Originally we sought closure simply by majority vote. Then, throughout most of the fifties, the battles turned on the question of whether the Senate was a "continuing body," with rules carried over from session to session, or whether each session could adopt new rules (and thus an altered closure rule). More recently these struggles have centered on a procedural ruling by the Vice-President.

In that first effort in 1949, when we were freshmen Senators, we were not only defeated; we were thrown for a loss. We started right out that January, as brand-new members of the Senate flushed with the victories in the Democratic convention and in the election, to change the Senate's Rule XXII so that a majority (instead of a two-thirds vote) could close off debate. President Truman supported us all the way. But when the smoke of battle lifted, the combination of Republican Senators with Southern Democrats and small-state Western Democrats had actually made closure a little *harder* than it had been before.

President Truman sent up a civil rights program consisting of measures for an FEPC, and against lynching, the poll tax, and segregation in transportation—all of which would have redeemed our party pledge in Philadelphia. But when we lost the fight over Rule XXII, we lost all serious chance to pass Mr. Truman's program.

In the fifties we tried to argue that each session of the Senate was a new body, free to adopt its own rules —and therefore free to adopt, by a simple majority vote, a new, more liberal closure rule. We lost all those fights, although this time in the end we did get the existing closure rule faintly liberalized. Lyndon Johnson, the majority leader, beat us, finally, in 1959, but mixed in with the defeat was the slight concession that closure could be invoked by two-thirds of those present and voting instead of two-thirds of the membership whether present or not. Although that change would make no difference in the historic closure vote in 1964, when all hundred Senators were present anyway, it was to make the crucial difference between victory and defeat in 1968.

The Act of 1957

Meanwhile, though, we did manage to pass a civil rights law without having a filibuster.

By the summer of 1957 the slow pace of school de-segregation had led to mounting pressure for a civil rights bill. After Mr. Eisenhower's re-election in 1956, his Attorney General, Herbert Brownell, deftly managed to get a bill sent to Congress as the proposal of the Eisenhower administration. It passed the House and was sent to the Senate in the summer of 1957. The Republican minority leader, William Knowland, joined by Paul Douglas, initiated an unusual and successful parliamentary action to by-pass Senator Eastland's Judiciary Committee (which had never reported out any civil rights bills). Knowland's move put the bill directly on the Senate calendar. Then, through a long summer, Lyndon Johnson worked out the compromises that made it possible to pass the Civil Rights Act of 1957—the first since Reconstruction. This Act was passed without a full-fledged filibuster. Although it was not a very strong law, its symbolic importance was great. It was the beginning.

The bill as it came from the House proposed to establish a Civil Rights Commission (my old "controversial" idea now became tame and acceptable) and to take steps to insure Negro voting rights. It also would have allowed the Attorney General to initiate suits in civil rights cases. This last point was the most controversial part. We liberals wanted this power for the Attorney General because the enforcement of the Supreme Court's 1954 school segregation was moving so slowly through the tedious court procedures. Individual Negroes in parts of the South had to be very brave to bring suit against segregated school systems. When they did so, there would be long delays and many evasions. This proposed "Part III" would allow the Department of Justice to bring suits on its own in these recalcitrant districts.

But for the same reason that we liberals wanted it, the segregationists feared and resisted it. When Majority Leader Johnson was working out the compromise by which he could pass the bill in the Senate, he soon discovered that the Southerners could never let this Part III of the House bill go by without a filibuster. It was Johnson's conviction that he could not get the votes to enact closure, and I think most observers who knew the Senate agreed that that was true. So in order to have any bill at all, there had to be a compromise with Richard Russell and the South. That meant that Part III had to be taken out; the Southerners also wanted a "jury trial" amendment—of symbolic significance mainly—put in. Lyndon Johnson said to me: "Well, which is it going to be? Do you liberals want to demagogue or do you want a bill?"

I wanted a bill, and other liberals did, and I agreed with Johnson's assessment of the power situation in the Senate: we could not have enacted closure that year, so he had to negotiate with Senator Russell and the segregationists. That a bill was passed at all was a reflection of the majority leader's skill.

But Part III was lost for the time being. It was revived and passed in the Civil Rights Act of 1964.

The Lessons of 1960

There was criticism, some by activists, of the compromise by which the 1957 Act was passed. Some felt that a Southern filibuster could have been beaten. In 1960, however, we found out that the threat of a filibuster was—unfortunately—all too real.

By that year the Senate, as a result of Northern Democratic victories in the 1958 elections, had become much more liberal than it had been before. We seemed to be in a better position for strong legislation than we had ever been. Ironically, our stronger position also strengthened the determination of the Southerners to resist *any* civil rights bill, lest this new, more liberal, Senate put over something especially objectionable. There was a long filibuster against the proposed civil rights bill, with all-night sessions and sleeping cots in the Senate cloakroom. The purpose of the round-the-clock sessions was to exhaust the filibusterers, but the Southern forces were better organized than we liberals were, and the strategy did not work.

Senator Russell had divided his segregationist troops into three teams of six Senators each, with each team successively taking about a six-hour turn of floor duty while the others rested. The absent Southerners didn't answer the quorum calls, so that whenever a Senator "suggested the absence of a quorum" we had civil rights Senators to produce from our own ranks the fifty-one present voters (for a quorum) to keep the Senate in session. The result was that our forces were more nearly exhausted than the filibusterers were. The strain of this and other pressures caused many civil rights activists to press for a vote on closure earlier than Johnson thought we had any chance of winning it. Without his support, an attempt at closure was made, and lost badly: the filibuster resumed; our momentum was lost; positions had hardened. We waited for the weak House bill and finally just passed that. It did little but add a new wrinkle to the voting provisions of the 1957 bill.

We learned valuable lessons from the 1960 fight that we were to apply in 1964: organize thoroughly; be ready at all times for quorum calls; and don't attempt closure until you can pass it. Also, we did not attempt the round-the-clock strategy.

So far as the composition of the Senate was concerned, we had as good a chance for strong civil rights legislation in 1960 as in 1964. But our strategy was going to be much better in 1964 than it had been in 1960. And we would have strong presidential backing, which we lacked in 1960. And—by far the most important fact—the attitude of the public by the later date was very different. The Senate of course does not act in a vacuum.

Meanwhile, in 1962, with John Kennedy now President, there was an attempt to get a very minimal bill dealing with literacy tests (a device often used to prevent Negroes from being registered to vote). This attempt failed entirely. There was no bill whatsoever, as a result of an effective Southern filibuster. Two efforts to enact closure failed badly, and the bill was shelved.

In 1964 the story would be very different, as I will indicate in the next chapter. But—to jump ahead to finish the filibuster story—the effort to change the closure rule still has not been victorious. The recent struggles have dealt with this question: whether the motion to adopt new rules, at the start of a Senate session, may *itself* be subjected to a filibuster. At the center of this battle is the ruling of the presiding officer (the Vice-President) when a motion to adopt new rules is made: Does he rule on that motion himself, or does he refer the matter back to the Senate for decision? This is a complicated and technical matter but an important one.

In 1967 I was the Vice-President who had to make this decision. The previous Vice-President, Lyndon Johnson, had referred the matter to the Senate's own debate; that decision had subjected the matter to the filibuster and hence had killed it. Richard Nixon, the Vice-President who had preceded Lyndon Johnson, had twice issued "advisory opinions" more favorable to the anti-filibuster forces—once in response to a parliamentary inquiry I made from the floor myself—but he had never been called upon actually to make the ruling.

In 1967, as Vice-President now myself, I did make a ruling and I took a position different from both of these previous Vice-Presidents. My own convictions were quite clear: that it should be easier to enact closure. At the same time, anyone who has absorbed the spirit of the Senate knows the importance of its tradition of ruling itself. The Vice-President—even though he be a former Senator (as the last five Vice-Presidents have been)—is an outsider, a member of the executive branch, not a Senator. To impose one man's views, one "outsider's" views, on the entire Senate, would have been a very serious and dubious act, and would have led to strong resistance. As a former Senator, I felt the force of the Senate's strong tradition of independence and of ruling itself. But at the same time I didn't want

just to turn the question back to the Senate to be fili-
bustered to death—as Vice-President Johnson had done
—either. I didn't want to lose this opportunity to advance the long battle against the filibuster. So—with
the help of researchers in the Library of Congress, my
staff and I found an obscure technicality which had the
full prestige of earlier statements by Senator Russell
himself, by which I could turn the question back to the
Senate in such a way as to allow for decision by the
Senate itself but by a series of undebatable *majority*
(not two-thirds) votes. If the anti-filibuster forces
could have held a simple majority intact, they could
have won. As it happened, they could not.

But it was the first time in history the United States
Senate could have ruled itself by a simple majority, if
it had wanted to. And my ruling now stands as a precedent for the Senate and the Vice-Presidents of the
future.

4

The Extraordinary Coalition
of 1964

In the forenoon of Wednesday, June 10, 1964, I sat at my desk in the front row of the United States Senate, listening carefully to a roll-call vote. I had done that many times before, but this roll call was unique. Nothing in my experience could quite match that extraordinary day. For the first time in American history we were going to enact closure on a civil rights bill. That meant we could shut off the filibuster and pass a strong measure. For a full year this bill had been before Congress; for ten years the nation had been struggling with the meaning of civil rights. This day was going to be the climax of the new movement for civil rights that had been mounting in intensity since World War II. The galleries were full; every Senator was present; the chamber was hushed; CBS had its camera set up out on the Capitol grounds and was tallying our votes, and the whole nation was watching us.

The bills we had passed in 1957 and 1960 had to be restricted to what the Southern Senators would allow to come to a vote. Now, in 1964, we had the chance to enact closure and therefore to pass a bill including fair employment, a "Powell amendment" provision (cutting off federal funds from programs that discriminate), and a section allowing the Attorney General to intervene in civil rights suits. These were the most difficult and important items left over from our civil rights battles in the past. In addition, we could outlaw discrimination in public accommodations. We could improve the protection of voting rights, and take a number of other forward steps.

We could do all this fundamentally because the attitude and the focus of attention of the entire nation had changed during the 1960's. The sit-in movement, the freedom rides, the widespread new commitment of Negroes, youth, and churchmen, and the fresh determination of the new Kennedy administration, had made the nation aware of the still unfulfilled promise of equality. The violence at Oxford, Mississippi, in September, 1962, when James Meredith was enrolled in the university, and then the violence in Alabama in the spring of 1963, had shocked the nation with the ugliness of the resistance. Americans all over the nation in April and May of 1963 saw pictures of the police dogs and fire hoses of the Birmingham police force attacking innocent Negroes. President Kennedy made a historic address to the nation, almost exactly a year to the day before this closure vote in the Senate, and put the full prestige of the Presidency behind the moral necessity of desegregation and civil rights. Shortly thereafter he had sent a comprehensive civil rights bill to Congress. It had been worked over in the House of Representatives, and actually strengthened, throughout the rest of 1963. It was reported by the House committee in November just two days before the tragic murder in Dallas.

When the new President, Lyndon Johnson, addressed a somber Congress and nation on the Wednesday after the assassination he appealed for the passage of the civil rights bill in the memory of the late President: "No memorial or eulogy could more eloquently honor President Kennedy than the earliest possible passage of the civil rights bill for which he fought so long." The memory of the young President who had proposed the bill and shock at his death were an important part of the background of the work that proceeded on this historic legislation. In one moving moment during the debate later on in the Senate— all the more touching because of what has happened since—Senator Edward Kennedy of Massachusetts closed his maiden Senate speech with these words: "My brother was the first President of the United States to state publicly that segregation was morally wrong. His heart and soul are in this bill . . ."

The House passed the bill in the February following the assassination, and the stage was set for the remarkable drama in the Senate, where so many civil rights proposals before it had died.

We had learned our lessons from the compromises of 1957 and 1960, the defeat of 1962, and our lack of success in the efforts to change Rule XXII. This time we had the people with us. A lot of history happened during the many months this Act was in formation: outrages in Birmingham, a great presidential speech, a tremendous march in Washington, the assassination of a young President—and more. This time the country was watching and ready. This time, in the Senate, we were very carefully organized.

As the House was completing its work on the bill in early 1964, the majority leader of the Senate, Mike Mansfield, asked me to be the floor leader when the bill came over to the Senate. Usually the chairman of the relevant committee acts as floor leader on a bill, but Mississippi's Senator James Eastland, chairman of the Judiciary Committee, obviously was not the appropriate leader for a civil rights bill. Sometimes the majority leader himself is the floor leader on a major piece of legislation like this one, but Senator Mansfield preferred it otherwise, keeping himself free in order to fulfill his other Senate duties.

I was glad to have the assignment. I appreciated it, and I looked upon it as the culmination of the struggle which had been going on ever since the convention of 1948 to pass civil rights legislation of this scope in the United States Senate. I was glad Senator Mansfield and other governmental leaders felt I was the man to do it. At the same time I knew this assignment would be a real test. I canceled the engagements on my calendar and worked full time on this one bill. Although I was hopeful through all those months, I also felt as though I were walking across very thin ice. A parliamentary situation can change very suddenly and go wrong in lots of different ways—especially in as delicate a maneuver as enacting closure on a civil rights bill in the Senate.

But I was determined that this time we were going to be thoroughly organized. During the fifties, when we were weak, and even during the Kennedy administration, when we lost many battles, there was a widespread notion—especially in the press—that the liberals in the Senate were "disorganized." Sometimes we had been. This time, I assured myself, it would be different. Organization, morale, and momentum are very important in a legislative battle—important in their effect both on your own forces and on the opposition. I was gratified to read in the press (this one from the *New York Times*): "Civil rights forces, not to be outdone by Southern opponents, have thrown up their own well-manned command post in the Senate . . . As militarily precise as the Southerners' three-platoon system, the Humphrey forces are organized down to the last man."

For this strong a bill we had to have closure, because the segregationists were dead set against it, and would filibuster endlessly. But closure is *very* hard to enact. By Senate rules it requires a two-thirds vote of those present—67 votes if all 100 Senators are in the chamber, as they almost certainly would be. That is a large order. This meant we had to develop an extraordinarily broad nation-wide coalition.

We knew, of course, that it had to be bipartisan. Senator Kuchel of California was the Republican floor leader for this bill, and he and I worked together as partners throughout those months. We had no significant disagreements, and sometimes the two of us would stand together against the Senate leaders of both parties, who understandably were slightly less committed to closure and a strong bill than we were.

Kuchel was committed from the start. But the key both to bipartisan cooperation and to closure—therefore to a strong bill—was to obtain the commitment of the Republican Senate leader, Everett Dirksen of Illinois. From the start, as the Democratic floor manager of the bill, I was determined to work with him. His support was essential. A major part of the delicate negotiation we carried on throughout the long months of the spring of 1964 concerned Senator Dirksen's proposed changes in the bill that the House had passed. In my first TV appearance during that struggle, on *Meet the Press,* I predicted that Senator Dirksen would support a strong bill (he was then saying he would not). I said that he would look upon this issue as a moral issue and not as a partisan issue. I knew that it was impossible to pass a civil rights bill without Senator Dirksen, because we had to have his help to get closure.

Every effort was made to involve him. I visited with him, encouraged him to take a more prominent role, asked him what changes he wanted to propose, urged him to call meetings and discuss his changes. He was opposed at first to the compulsory enforcement powers in the public-accommodations section. He also was opposed to an FEPC. He had his doubts about Title VI, which cut off federal funds where there was discrimination. But we worked with him, and we went over the bill very carefully with his staff. We held many meetings in his office. He had a great sheaf of proposed amendments, but in the end he gave a good deal of ground. The bill which he finally supported is, in my mind, as good or better than the House bill. He insisted mainly on some time for conciliation and more involvement of local and state government, both of which were very good ideas, and I supported them.

I was told a number of times by Democrats that

Dirksen was stealing the show. Many of my party associates thought that, as the leader, the meetings should have been held in my office rather than in his office. I said: "Listen, I don't care where we meet. I'll meet any place with Dirksen and he can have all meetings in his office. I'll come." And I said: "If this thing fails, none of you guys will want to be around me. You're a very lonely fellow in defeat. I'll take all the onus for its failure. If it passes, there will be glory enough for everybody." I told Senator Dirksen: "Everett, very frankly we can't pass this bill without you. I want to work with you." I never made a move without consulting him.

And in the end we were able to put together a strong bill—including changes he proposed—that both he and I could support, and we got the votes for closure that he could influence.

Working closely with Senator Dirksen was one part of our strategy. Keeping our civil rights forces well organized was another.

We put out a daily newssheet, which was certainly an innovation. In it we summarized the proceedings and gave the civil rights' forces answers to the arguments of the opposition.

One day, on the floor, Senator Stennis of Mississippi inquired about this newsletter. "I should like to ask," he said, "who writes these mysterious messages which come to Senators before the *Congressional Record* reaches them, and . . . attempts to refute arguments made on the floor of the Senate . . ."

I was glad he asked. It gave me a chance to publicize our organizational efforts.

"There is no doubt about it," I said. "The newsletter is a bipartisan civil rights newsletter . . . For the first time we are putting up a battle. Everything will be done to make us succeed . . . I wish also to announce that if anyone wishes to have equal time, there is space on the back of it for the opposition . . ."

We had to cooperate as Republicans and Democrats. We had to work together as liberals, moderates, and conservatives. We had to maintain close and favorable relations with "the other house" (the House of Representatives) lest their rejection of our changes in the bill force a conference, and thus another vote, and thus another filibuster.

We developed a quorum duty system, with a daily list of Senators from both parties who were on duty for quorum calls. We divided our supporters into small groups, with a captain for each group. (We had people on the floor every hour of the day. A man was responsible for so many hours. He had to produce so many Senators for a quorum call.) Through this entire long period, from the middle of February to the middle of June, we failed to produce a quorum only once —and when that happened we publicized the names of those who had been absent, and that was the end of that. In 1960 the Southerners had hurt us badly with repeated quorum calls, but in 1964 we were organized and we had the matter licked.

The unwavering support of the President was essential to keep Senators in line and to convince our opponents that we were, and would continue to be, firm and serious. We had to work closely with others in the executive branch, especially with Attorney General

Robert Kennedy and his colleagues in the Justice Department, to test the technicalities of the complicated titles and amendments. I asked Mr. Kennedy to assign Mr. Katzenbach to work with us, and the Justice Department officials spent hours on technical changes in the bill.

We had to keep the debate on a high and serious level, with no personal attacks or invective, and to maintain good relations with our opponents (uncommitted Senators could be offended if we did not). We dealt with Senator Richard Russell of Georgia, the Southern leader, and his colleagues with fairness and careful courtesy. We assured them that we would not try to win by parliamentary tricks. I went out of my way to maintain good personal relations with the Southern Senators, even while we were arguing with each other constantly on the floor. During this period, in fact, Senator Willis Robertson of Virginia became a friend of mine. Nearing the point of recess on a day in March, for example, after he had just made a speech ridiculing every title of the bill and I had answered him, he walked over to me on the Senate floor and offered me a Confederate flag for my lapel. I accepted the flag as graciously as I could, and I praised Senator Robertson not only for his "eloquence and his great knowledge of history and law, but also for his wonderful . . . gentlemanly qualities and his consideration to us at all times."

Senator Robertson then responded to me with a Virginian's ultimate compliment: "I told the Senator [meaning me] that if it had not been for the men from Wisconsin and Minnesota, when Grant finally came down into Virginia, we would have won. But they formerly belonged to Virginia. We could not whip them . . ."

Senator Robertson and I then left the floor arm in arm, and retired to my office for a drink.

We divided the responsibility for defending the sections of the bill among many Senators, to broaden the involvement and the credit. Senators Clark, Magnuson, Hart, and others were made team captains for particular titles of the bill.

We had regular meetings, and we set up a research center and a command center. Even though we had all been through many debates on some similar bills before, we carefully presented our case once again, answering every argument, developing every point.

We took the offensive early—before we had really planned to—in order to keep the Southerners from dominating the news. We wanted to get our case to the press; on the whole we had good treatment from the news media.

I opened the debate on the bill itself with a complete statement, which took some three hours; Senator Kuchel followed. Each day a team of our people would take a title, so that for more than twelve days we held the floor. We gave out detailed information; we let the public know what was in the bill and why it should pass.

We encouraged the Senators on our side to go on radio and television. I wrote to each Senator, suggesting television programs, suggesting newsletters for the folks back home, and enclosing sample copies of newsletters other Senators had prepared. We encouraged reprints of key material, so that people would know the answers to the arguments. We answered the propaganda of the anti-civil rights groups.

The Republicans had team captains under Senator Kuchel, corresponding to our Democratic set. Two or three of the Republicans were not deeply committed, and even opposed certain sections of the bill—Senators Hruska of Nebraska and Cotton of New Hampshire. They asked to be relieved of their duties. But most stayed on. Senators Scott, Keating, Javits, Allott, and Cooper, along with Senator Kuchel, were especially important among the Republicans.

When the several Senators got a chance to be their party's team captains for the different titles of the bill, they got some press for themselves and became known as among those fighting for civil rights. They became more engaged.

We had our meetings at the Capitol every morning, half an hour before the session—at 9:30 or 10:30. We determined after our 1960 experience that it would do little or no good to have round-the-clock sessions; we preferred instead just to make the sessions long enough so that Senators (and eventually the public) would recognize that their time was being frittered away.

Other Senate business, of course, was stalled while the filibuster continued, and pressure to end it grew. The heavy barrage of newsletters going out from our Senators pointed out that all this talking was wasting time. The refusal of the Southern Senators to allow any voting—except in one or two instances on minor amendments—contributed to the mounting exasperation with the filibuster. Frankly, I was rather surprised at the Southerners' tactics. I never could quite understand why they didn't let us vote more often. If they had done so, they could have insisted that the legislative process after all was working, because amendments were being voted upon. But they didn't do that. Instead they just kept talking and talking. It seemed to me that they had lost their sense of direction and had little or no plan other than what they used to have when filibusters succeeded.

I think the truth is that in that year—in contrast to some other years—we just had a lot better organization and morale than did the segregationists.

Our plan, of course, was to try to make the growing annoyance with the filibuster work to our advantage —toward votes for closure, instead of toward compromise on the content of the bill.

We kept a good spirit throughout, even on the most difficult days. There was little acrimony and few signs of temper. For my part, I made the most strenuous effort to keep it that way. That may sound like a minor matter, but in a delicate parliamentary situation that counts. I can even remember talking, literally, to myself, when I was assigned to be floor manager of the bill. I had to make up my mind how I would conduct myself. I was determined to keep my patience. I told myself not to lose my temper, no matter how outrageous I thought the arguments might be. I wanted to try to preserve a reasonable degree of good nature and fair play in the Senate. I think we succeeded.

We knew that our coalition had to transcend ideological lines, and that it had to reach out in an extraordinary way beyond Capitol Hill and beyond the Washington pressure groups to great segments of the American public that rarely pay attention to the daily activities of the United States Senate.

We had to have the votes of far more than the committed civil rights liberals in the Senate, and more than the moderates. For the two-thirds vote for closure we needed the votes of conservatives who had grave reservations about extending federal power, and of Senate traditionalists very reluctant ever to vote for limiting debate. Therefore, we had to develop an unusually broad national alliance and an unusually deep national commitment—a moral commitment, transcending the ordinary arguments of politics.

It is a terrible fact that the barrier of the filibuster allowed an intransigent minority to block for so long the laws against racial discrimination that should have been enacted many, many years before. But—making a virtue of necessity—we may say this: the need to develop the extraordinary depth and breadth required to enact closure in the Senate made the passage of this Civil Rights Act of 1964 truly a *national* action, reflecting a broad American consensus on the most fundamental of American ideals, to a degree that is rarely true of pieces of legislation.

We had to have strong support from across the country. We worked closely with the remarkable Leadership Conference on Civil Rights, which mobilized a broad range of civil rights groups, labor groups, liberals, religious people, business leaders, and others. There were meetings all across the nation. The civil rights groups that before this and again after this would often be at odds cooperated fully during those important months. So did diverse liberal and labor groups. And a wide spectrum of religious groups, of many faiths, cooperated to give the most important public support to the bill.

We had decided very early that the religious groups had to play a large role in supporting this measure. Early in March we met with representatives of the three faiths, in my office, and selected the date April 28 for the interfaith civil rights convocation to be held at Georgetown University (it was in this struggle of 1964, by the way, that the three faiths really began to work together in a significant large-scale way). We designed plans for civil rights meetings across the country, with the clergy taking the lead. Protestant, Catholic, and Jewish seminarians, working together, maintained a silent twenty-four-hour vigil on the Capitol grounds throughout the long Senate debate. Delegation after delegation of clergymen and church people quietly visited Senators. Without the clergy we could never have passed the bill.

In a kind of reverse compliment that is impressive because it comes from the opposition, Senator Russell said this in his closing speech: "I have observed with profound sorrow the role that many religious leaders have played in urging the passage of the bill . . . During the course of the debate we have seen cardinals, bishops, elders, stated clerks, common preachers, priests, and rabbis come to Washington to press for passage of the bill . . . day after day, men of the cloth have been standing on the Mall and urging a favorable vote on the bill. They have encouraged and prompted thousands of good citizens to sign petitions in support of the bill . . ."

The support of religious leaders was especially important for these reasons: because it was both right and strategically necessary to emphasize the moral dimension of this issue, transcending the ordinary argument of party and political philosophy; because religious communities could reach the hinterlands (which were difficult for liberal-labor-Negro groups to reach), whose Senators were decisive for our closure vote; and because it was imperative that our efforts be a dignified and serious appeal to conscience, rather than anything that looked like intimidation (legislators, understandably, are very sensitive about efforts to coerce their vote).

Labor groups were very important, too. Andrew Beimiller, who is now lobbyist for the AFL-CIO, was right there with us throughout that spring, helping to finish what we had started together back in 1948. Joe Rauh, the ADA leader, was there with us, too, as co-chairman of the Leadership Conference. And Paul Douglas was in the Senate.

We had daily strategy meetings, and more than a hundred private meetings with visiting groups of supporters. We developed in those months of 1964 one of the most extraordinary coalitions in the history of American politics. And now, on June 10, it was coming to its great test.

I was confident about the outcome. We had held off any effort to enact closure until we felt we could win, because to have tried and failed would have been a serious setback, bringing upon us irresistible pressures to dilute the bill and compromise with the resistant segregationists. So we had to win. We had counted the votes many times. I had called President Johnson the night before to assure him that we would win. And one more time that night, for a final insurance, I phoned three Senators—Edmundson, Yarborough, and Cannon —whose votes were not certain. I anticipated victory. An hour before the vote I gave Senator Hart a note that said we would get sixty-nine (we got seventy-one).

But still you never can be absolutely certain until you actually hear the votes, and so I was listening very carefully and checking my list vote by vote. Every single Senator was there that day—even Senator Clair Engle of California, dying of a brain tumor and unable to speak, who was wheeled into the chamber and voted "Aye" by pointing to his eye. Senator Carl Hayden, the oldest member of the Senate, who has represented Arizona ever since it became a state and who on principle has never voted to limit debate, waited in the cloakroom to see whether his vote would be needed. The Senate chamber, of course, was packed, hushed, filled with a dramatic tension beyond anything even the most senior Senators had experienced. As the votes were cast, my confidence rose, because we were getting every vote we had counted on, and one or two besides. When I heard the sixty-seventh "Aye," involuntarily I raised my arms over my head, in a gesture of deep satisfaction.

For me, personally, it was the culmination of the full year's fight for the Civil Rights Act, of fifteen years' battle for civil rights in the United States Senate, and of a lifetime in politics in which equal opportunity had been the objective above all others. For the small band of Senate liberals it was a full victory at last, after years of frustration, defeat, and compromise. For the civil rights forces in the nation it was the climax not only of the extraordinary coalition of the spring of 1964, but also of the extraordinary civil rights decade since the Supreme Court's school segregation decision in 1954, and of more than half a century of devoted work.

On June 10, after the longest filibuster in history, we did enact closure. We went on to pass the Civil Rights Act of 1964 itself on Friday, June 19. To tell the truth, we had concentrated and organized so much for the closure fight that we were not as well prepared as we should have been for this legislative period after closure was enacted, when each Senator was limited to one hour. We had to cross some slippery territory, with amendments and parliamentary tactics and some breaking up of our forces—but we made it.

I do not remember much of the last days of the debate, for a personal reason. Two days before its finish I was called off the Senate floor to take a telephone call from my wife in Minnesota, who told me that our second son, Robert, had a malignant growth in his throat. He had to go through two operations, one a massive procedure to clean out the whole lymphatic system. I was simply paralyzed. After she talked to me I had a hard time going back onto the Senate floor. Arguments you can listen to without emotion when you are calm become much harder to take when you are under a personal strain. But I had to stay there until the end of the debate and the passage of the bill before flying to Minnesota.

The boy recovered fully in the weeks of the summer.

After the final passage of the Act a number of us gathered in Majority Leader Mansfield's office; when a few Senators left after an hour they found a crowd of several thousand persons circling the Senate wing of the Capitol, waiting to cheer and congratulate them. When I finally left, a full three hours later, I was astonished and touched to find that there was still a crowd of several hundred persons encamped outside, waiting all that time just to cheer the leaders of the Senate's effort. Never in my fifteen years in the Senate, nor in the memory of Senators with a far longer period of service than mine, had there been anything like it. The public was involved in that legislative battle in a way that was unique.

On June 19 the Senate passed the bill. The House then approved the Senate revisions without sending the bill to committee (that was important). And then, on July 2, the President signed into law the Civil Rights Act of 1964.

5

The Civil Rights Acts

The most widely discussed section of the Civil Rights Act prohibited discrimination in public accommodations. It killed Jim Crow, or at least, mortally wounded him. The "Strange Career of Jim Crow"—strange and terrible—at last was ended.

To a later generation, looking back, it may appear a small thing that a Negro could not legally be barred from a hotel or a restaurant or gas-station restroom or a movie theater or a lunch counter. But to those who had had to live with that Jim Crow system, who had known what it meant to drive extra miles for a room or gas, to be denied admittance to movies and plays, to be shut out of hotels and eating places—for them it was no small matter. You say a cup of coffee at a lunch counter does not mean very much? It does if you are *denied* it because of your color. To repeat, the essence of the Jim Crow system was not separation but subordination—it was humiliation, indignity, assigning people to a "place." Therefore, it was at the very heart of the injustice toward a race.

Today in Birmingham, Alabama, where the repressive action of the white police had once shocked the nation, Negroes eat at the restaurants, stay in the hotels, and go to the theaters in a matter-of-fact way that not long ago the residents of that city would have found hard to believe. As Vice-President, I have been in all fifty states. I have attended racially integrated meetings in the heart of the South, in hotels and restaurants that once were strictly segregated. I spoke at a breakfast in Oxford, Mississippi, attended by the brother of Medgar Evers and the brother of Ross Barnett. In that regard, at least, it is a new day.

But the public accommodations section was very far from being the only part of the 1964 Act. Another was Title VI, the powerful section which requires that federal funds be denied to any activity that engages in racial discrimination or segregation. Hospitals, schools, welfare programs, public housing, libraries, and many other public activities can be integrated through this provision.

This part of the Act has taken on added significance as we have developed all the federal aid programs of recent years. In order to get the federal money a state or a school district must comply with this title of the Act—and the denial of those funds can be a powerful lever. It is from this title that the "guidelines" of the Department of Health, Education and Welfare have resulted—"guidelines" of compliance with Title VI of the Act. Recently HEW has issued a new set of regulations that will apply to the de facto segregation of many school districts of the *North,* as well as the South. Resistance to the "guidelines" has been strong; in the past year, though, compliance and acceptance have increased greatly. Local communities are coming to understand that the HEW officials are carrying out the law of the land, the will of the American people as expressed in the Civil Rights Act of 1964.

The two parts of the Act that had the longest and

most checkered history, and that were the main symbols of a "strong" bill, were "Part III," as it was called in the 1957 bill, and the old FEPC, now called the Equal Employment Opportunity Commission (EEOC).

"Part III," you will remember, was the section of the bill passed by the House in 1957 that would have given the Attorney General power to intervene to protect a citizen's constitutional rights. It was dropped in the Senate that year as part of the compromise that got the 1957 bill passed without a filibuster. Now in 1963 and 1964 that provision was revived. And alongside it was an equal employment provision.

Back in the spring and early summer of 1963 we had many meetings on what should go into the Kennedy administration's new civil rights bill. Some of these meetings were in Majority Leader Mansfield's office, some at the White House, some at the Department of Justice. In May we began to bring the results of these meetings into our regular Tuesday morning congressional leaders' breakfast with President Kennedy. There were arguments especially about whether to include equal employment and the grant of power to the Attorney General. I argued for the strong and comprehensive bill, including these parts, but it was finally decided that they should be omitted. The administration feared that a stronger bill would run into trouble in the House Rules Committee and in the Senate. I had talks in early June with President Kennedy and with his chief speechwriter, Ted Sorensen, about the President's message, and I urged them to include equal employment in the message at least if not in the proposed bill itself. It was only a few hours before the message came to Congress that they decided to do this.

Then in the House the provision allowing the Attorney General's intervention was added by the Judiciary Committee, and the EEOC was added on the House floor. We liberals were pleased that the House took this action, because it would have been difficult (really, impossible) to *add* strong sections in the Senate. We were going to have a hard enough time passing whatever the House sent down. Republican William McCullogh of Ohio deserves much credit for the House's crucial action; so does Charles Halleck, then the Republican leader in the House, and—once more—President Kennedy, for his quiet work persuading Halleck.

When President Kennedy was shot in November and Lyndon Johnson became President, there was doubt in some quarters about what the new President would do with the bill, which would soon be moving to the Senate. President Johnson made clear in his very first statement that he would actively support its passage—as the highest priority and as a memorial to the slain President. But some—remembering his compromise of 1957—wondered whether he would support the entire "strong" bill, or would drop EEOC or Title VI or the enforceable public accommodations section. But I did not doubt that he would support it in its entirety, and I urged him to do so. He did. We both knew that 1963–64 was very different from 1957, and that this time we had a chance to pass the complete package. And that is what we did.

Discrimination in Employment—and Full Employment

We kept equal employment in the Senate bill. Thus the Act did something for which we had been fighting since World War II, since the Democratic platform of 1948 and the Truman civil rights proposals: it made racial discrimination in employment against the law of the land. Title VII of the Civil Rights Act of 1964 created—at last—a federal agency for equal employment opportunity.

In the long negotiations with Senator Dirksen and the conservative Republicans we had given room to the state FEPC's in the twenty-five states in which they existed, and we had placed added reliance on efforts to obtain voluntary compliance. Nevertheless the law does flatly prohibit discrimination or segregation. It applies to employers, to labor unions (which may not lawfully exclude persons on racial grounds), to employment agencies, to job-training programs, to employment advertising. It prohibits all sorts of discrimination—in hiring, in pay, in upgrading, in conditions of work. The law applied at first just to firms employing a hundred or more; it has just now (in 1968) finished moving progressively through stages to cover all those employing twenty-five or more.

The agency set up by this part of the Act—the "Equal Employment Opportunity Commission"—has power not only to hear complaints but also to make investigations. It has held hearings recently, for example, on discrimination in white-collar employment in New York City.

Why aren't there more Negroes and members of other minority groups in these central offices of America's businesses—in New York corporation headquarters, in finance (banking, insurance, brokerage), and in communications (radio-TV, advertising, publishing)? And why are there even fewer in the field offices of these major companies?

The Equal Employment Opportunity Commission needs enforcement powers of its own, so that it can issue "cease and desist" orders and thus be still more effective. But it is not our only tool for fair employment. There has also been a requirement of equal opportunity employment in firms doing business with the government—"contract compliance" as it is called. It is a powerful tool. If a firm wants that contract to make army gloves, it has to show affirmative action to employ minorities. John F. Kennedy created, by executive order in 1961, a President's Committee on Equal Employment Opportunity, which required "affirmative action" for minority employment (not just routine statements of non-discrimination) on the part of firms doing business with the government. In 1963 President Kennedy issued another executive order broadening the application of the requirement to cover all firms engaged in private construction projects using federal funds. In 1965, after we passed the Civil Rights Act of 1964 and the EEOC came into being, President Johnson renamed this earlier effort the "Office of Contract Compliance" and located it in the Department of Labor.

The laws in all these fields cast their light before them into voluntary and private actions. In the employment field there are groups like Project Equality, under which the churches use their great purchasing power, as the federal government has done, to promote affirmative action for equal opportunity among firms with which they do business. In Plans for Progress, a group of business leaders work voluntarily for equal employment opportunity. The National Alliance of Businessmen, headed by Henry Ford II, is seeking out the hardcore unemployed person and trying to put him to work. As in Minneapolis twenty years ago, so today we need to combine strong laws and active government enforcement with voluntary, private efforts, persuasion, publicity, and conciliation.

Equal employment practices are a necessity—but they are not enough. There must also be enough jobs, and the right training, so the people who need them can fill the positions that are available. There must now also be a full employment program—work for all—with incentives to attract private business into the ghetto, where the unemployed are; and into the South, where rural people are thrown off the land; and incentives also to build workers' housing in the suburbs, where more and more industry is locating. We have to bring together the jobless and the jobs. We must consider having the government serve as an "employer of last resort." In the late fifties in the Senate, I was proposing a new version of the CCC of New Deal days—a government work-training program, especially for youth, that would do needed public tasks. Modified, this later became the neighborhood youth corps and job corps of the war on poverty. A more inclusive version, which actually provides the jobs, may be necessary if our present efforts fail to reach the hard-core unemployed in sufficient numbers.

In a later chapter I suggest that we should have a new humane and dignified system of welfare. But for all those who are able, work is far better than "welfare." Jobs for all is now the step we must take, to realize the promise begun by the fair employment provision of the Act of 1964.

Equal opportunity does not mean jobs alone, but also the chance to be promoted, and to be a professional, a self-employed person, an entrepreneur who employs others, a proprietor.

For the larger meaning of equal opportunity, positive new action is now required. Equal employment laws were the first step.

The Disenfranchisement of the Negro

Many citizens thought that the Act of 1964 brought to an end the legislative phase of the battle for civil rights. But less than a year later, after Alabama state troopers had attacked the marchers in Selma, President Johnson came before the new and more liberal Congress to ask for another major civil rights law, this one dealing with the right to vote.

For many years after the Civil War Negroes *did* vote. But then, in the late nineteenth century, when the North—the nation—turned away from its responsibility, white supremacists took away the Negro's vote—that most fundamental of all civil rights.

How did they do it? How *could* they do it, when not only the American democratic creed and way of life in general but also a particular constitutional amendment—the fifteenth—specifically affirmed that right? (That amendment says, plainly enough: "The right of citizens of the United States to vote shall not be denied or abridged by the United States or by any state on account of race, color or previous condition of servitude.'') The white supremacists were able to do this by a series of subterfuges, usually not explicitly based on racism but always reflecting it.

The poll tax was one device: since most ex-slaves were poor, they couldn't pay the tax. The abolition of the poll tax had been an objective of the Truman civil rights program and of bills offered by liberals like myself—I offered one as soon as I got to the Senate. The twenty-fourth amendment—declared in effect in January, 1964—and Court decisions have now outlawed that objectionable feature of our past.

The ''grandfather clauses'' that barred from voting those whose ancestors were slaves were struck down by the Supreme Court in cases beginning in 1915 (the NAACP's first major victory).

The most cynical device was the ''white primary'': nominations made in the Democratic Party primaries in the South have been equivalent to election—and these primaries were limited by state law to whites. When the Supreme Court declared those white primary laws unconstitutional in 1927, many Southern states declared the parties ''private clubs,'' which could discriminate as they wished; after an earlier decision accepted that subterfuge, the Supreme Court in 1944 declared it unconstitutional.

The striking down of these efforts to keep Negroes from voting by law was only the first battle in this war. As late as 1960 only four per cent of the Negro population of Mississippi was registered; again and again in a belt of counties across the South there were no Negroes registered, or only a handful. In many of the counties with very large numbers of Negro citizens the black voters were excluded almost completely from the voting rolls. This was effected by persistent flouting of their constitutional rights. Literacy requirements and many kinds of delay and evasion were used to keep Negroes from registering. Frequently there was economic retaliation against those brave enough to register, and in all too many cases there was violence.

Some brave and persistent Negroes nevertheless did get themselves registered—but should it be necessary for an American citizen to be a hero just to be registered to vote?

The 1957 Civil Rights Act was a beginning of the attempt to extend federal power, as a last resort, into the registering of voters. The results, however, were disappointing. The slight improvements made by the 1960 Act did not change the picture very much either: most Southern Negroes eligible to vote still were not on the lists.

Starting in 1963 a Voters Education Project set up by the major civil rights organizations began to help Southern Negroes to register, and there was some improvement. The resistance still was strong, and the numbers registered in the Deep South counties was small.

In the summer of 1964 numbers of college students and other concerned people went to Mississippi for the remarkable "Mississippi Summer Project," to register voters and build political strength among the Negroes of that state. The project, again, was sponsored by a wide coalition of civil rights groups of varying ideological hues, as we were to learn at that summer's Democratic convention.

The Mississippi Freedom Democratic Party

Knowing they would meet intransigent resistance from the regular Democratic Party, the civil rights workers in Mississippi formed a party of their own, the Mississippi Freedom Democratic Party, and elected their own slate of delegates—sixty-four Negroes and four whites—to the Democratic convention in Atlantic City in August, 1964. They challenged the all-white regular Democratic delegation. At the convention, where I was a possible choice for the vice-presidential nomination, we were confronted with this situation: a Mississippi "delegation" which had no legal standing whatever but did have a very strong *moral* case and had pledged itself to support the convention nominees and platform (members of the regular delegation might support Goldwater). The strength of the MFDP's moral case was made evident to the whole nation when its counsel, my old ADA friend Joseph Rauh, Jr., managed to get its testimony before the credentials committee carried on national television. That was the most important move in the complicated struggle over the Mississippi delegation at Atlantic City.

Two weeks before, it had appeared impossible and absurd to expect that the MFDP could win any actual seats at the convention. The ordinary delegate—not just the conservatives and segregationists—had felt that, after all, you couldn't have an ex post facto disqualification of a properly chosen delegation. Though many were sympathetic to the Mississippi Negro, they still felt that an aggrieved group couldn't just appoint itself as a delegation and try to supplant the legally chosen one. And most observers did not expect the MFDP delegation to get anything except perhaps the privilege of the convention floor, with no votes.

But the televised appearance of Fannie Lou Hamer and others of the MFDP made clear the strength of their moral case. The testimony was eloquent, dignified, moving—and shocking. It revealed to the nation how Negro voters were systematically and sometimes ruthlessly shut out of power in Mississippi. Indignation among delegates and the public was strong enough for us to obtain a settlement which went far beyond what anyone had thought realistically possible in the days before the convention. The Democratic Party pledged itself never again to allow deliberately segregated and unrepresentative delegations to be seated; the process of selecting delegates had to be open to all legally qualified persons. It required the regular Mississippi delegation to pledge support to the party ticket; those delegates who refused the loyalty oath were denied their seats. And—what nobody had really expected—it gave the MFDP two voting delegates-at-large. It was an impressive victory, although the radical group within the MFDP did not think so.

This settlement was worked out in an all-night meeting the first day of the convention—August 24, 1964. Walter Reuther of the UAW had flown in the middle of the night from Detroit, and he and I functioned as mediators between White House aides, liberal delegates, and conservative delegates. A great deal of the credit for the remarkable gains made in that meeting belongs to Reuther. Walter Mondale was also an important negotiator. I had recommended him. He was then Attorney General of Minnesota, a delegate from that state, and a man not as identified and tagged as I was.

Although the liberal delegates from many states accepted the settlement that we worked out that night, and Joe Rauh accepted it and Aaron Henry of the Mississippi NAACP at first did, an extreme group with the MFDP rejected it. They staged a sit-in at the convention. But their reaction should not obscure the fact that a considerable victory in fact was won at Atlantic City. The two voting delegates were symbolically important. The required pledge to support the ticket helped settle the aggravated "loyalty oath" question that had been around Democratic conventions since the walkout of 1948 (the question about delegations that voted in the convention on the party's nominee and then went home and supported somebody else in the election itself).

But by far the most important point is that the MFDP struggle ended the long history of lily-white delegations from the South. The real impact of the action taken in 1964 was evident in the convention of 1968, when the credentials committee recommended, and the convention accepted, these historic decisions: the seating of an entire challenging delegation from Mississippi because of the racial barriers which had been imposed in selecting the regular delegation; the seating of both the regular and the challenging delegations from Georgia, with the delegate votes divided between them; the requiring of Alabama and other challenged delegations that they subscribe in good faith not to support any nominees other than those selected by the convention—major steps in ridding the Democratic Party of racial discrimination. Anybody who saw J. Strom Thurmond and company angrily marching out of the Philadelphia convention hall in 1948 knows that this was indeed progress.

The Voting Rights Act

In November, 1964, President Johnson was re-elected by a very large margin over Barry Goldwater, who had voted dramatically against the Civil Rights Act in the previous June. I was elected Vice-President, and the Congress chosen in that election—the 89th Congress—was the most liberal in my lifetime.

In March a group of civil rights supporters started a march from Selma, Alabama, to the state capitol in Montgomery, to protest the repression of the efforts of the voters' education campaign. State troopers attacked the marchers with clubs and tear gas. Two days later a Unitarian minister was fatally beaten by a gang in Selma, and two weeks later Mrs. Viola Liuzzo of Detroit was shot down in her car.

Once again—as in 1963—the brutality of the resistance furnished the public support and indignation to spur legislation through Congress. President Johnson responded to the moment with the full powers of moral leadership of his office; he went before Congress and the public to ask for a bill to allow the federal government to register voters in the intransigent counties of the Deep South. In one of the most moving moments in recent American history this first modern President from the South took over as his own the civil rights workers' phrase "We shall overcome": "Their cause must be our cause, too. Because it's not just Negroes but really it's all of us who must overcome the crippling disease of bigotry and injustice. And we . . . shall . . . overcome.''

The Senate voted closure on a civil rights bill for the second time in history, and then passed the bill seventy-seven to nineteen, this time after only ten weeks' debate. In the House twenty-two Southerners joined the large majority in favor of it—a harbinger of the future that is coming. The President signed the bill into law in the President's room at the Capitol after addressing the nation from the rotunda.

This is the Act that has had the swiftest and most visible effect for the poor Negro of a Deep South town. Dining in a formerly segregated restaurant doesn't mean much to him, since he often does not have the money to go to the restaurant anyway. But the Voting Rights Act means that he can go to the post office, instead of the county courthouse, to register. He can register under federal protection, without hostility or intimidation.

It means that if he lives in Holmes County, Mississippi—just a few short years ago overwhelmingly dominated by white voters—he now has a Negro representative in the Mississippi state legislature. It means Negro candidates for sheriff (that most important office for the poor Southern Negro) and for the school board and even for Congress. (Charles Evers made a strong bid to become the first Negro Congressman from Mississippi.) It means that the white candidates have to pay attention to the black man's vote, treat him respectfully and listen to his wants.

In Mississippi, the most intransigent of segregationist states, there were only 35,000 Negroes registered before the Voting Rights Act of 1965; as I write, there are 264,000; and when you read this, there will be many more. In Georgia, Alabama, and South Carolina over fifty per cent of the eligible Negroes are registered; in Florida over sixty per cent. And registration continues to climb steadily without incident.

The vote does not solve everything, but it is an essential democratic beginning—a foundation for self-respect and peaceful power. The new interracial Southern politics—I predict —will soon become a source of political health for the nation as a whole. And in Northern cities growing numbers of Negro voters can form the base for a more responsive, more progressive city politics. I do not mean just by electing black leaders—but the election of Carl Stokes as Mayor of Cleveland and Richard Hatcher as Mayor of Gary, in the fall of 1967, represented black power at its best. It is also more than that: a new and better chapter in the unfolding story of American democracy.

Mayor Stokes, an extremely able and promising leader, graduated from the University of Minnesota law school; I have a soft spot for all those civil rights leaders whom Minnesota has contributed to the nation (we claim Roy Wilkins, too). I went to Cleveland in behalf of Carl Stokes back when he first ran in 1965, as an independent Democrat opposing the regular Democratic nominee. The party leadership in Cleveland —friends of mine—raised hell with me for that, but I said I had a right to meet with anyone I wanted to. I encouraged friends to contribute to Stokes' campaigns.

I was also co-chairman of a fund-raising party in New York for Richard Hatcher, which as Vice-President of the United States I had not done for any other man.

These are very able men. They are bringing to their cities the kind of leadership the cities need. Frankly, the fact that they are Negroes helps, and helps in lots of ways. It helps the black poor of the city to identify with city hall—and with its problems. It helps Negroes across the country to have hope. It teaches white citizens something important about equality and democracy. It begins to contradict the negative foreign propaganda about this country. But most important—these men are outstanding leaders.

The day will come—and I think it is coming fast— when we can ignore race and praise men like Mayor Stokes and Mayor Hatcher and Senator Edward Brooke and Mississippi leader Charles Evers and all the others strictly for their personal abilities. But in the meantime this nation will soon have many more Negro mayors and city councilmen and sheriffs and school board members and state legislators and Senators and Congressmen. That will come about because of the fundamental weapon of democracy—of citizen power—the vote.

After the Laws Are Passed

The enactment of closure and the passage of those acts in 1964–65 were the greatest legislative achievements of the civil rights movement—the movement that had been working, since World War II at least, for laws against racial discrimination,

And what did it all come to? In the light of what has

happened since, some now would discount these civil rights laws—and it is certainly obvious that they are a long way from being enough.

Sadly, they may even have accelerated our current black-white crises in the cities, by arousing higher hopes among blacks and also by giving uninformed whites the feeling that now the thing is settled. The very necessity to carry on such a long, intense nation-wide struggle may have led many to think that this legislation would do vastly more to transform race relations in this country.

This civil rights legislation has not brought full equality. It did not make the American Negro the free and equal citizen of the United States that he ought to be. It did not accomplish all that some of its supporters thought it would.

But neither was it the failure that some, in disillusionment, now think it is.

Too many Americans expected too much of civil rights laws. This is true, in different ways, of both the black and the white. In particular, some white Americans, of mild good will but other preoccupations, thought that the passage of these laws would solve the problem once and for all, and end the agitation. They thought the country could sigh with relief and turn to other matters. They have since become puzzled and angry that that didn't happen—that much more is needed, and that agitation for equal treatment has not stopped, but rather increased.

Other Americans, of a radical bent, have written off the older civil rights movement as a complete failure, because Negroes are still treated unfairly.

Still other Americans, never sympathetic to the aims

of the civil rights movement, now look back on it as a
dangerous opening wedge; they confuse peaceful demonstrations with riots, and believe that the civil rights
movement set the precedent for lawlessness and extremism.

I take a different view from all of these. I suggest
that we look upon the civil rights movement that produced the closure vote and those civil rights acts not as
a completed thing and an accomplished success, nor
on the other hand as a failure nor—certainly not—as a
dangerous precedent. Instead we can look at the laws
of that period positively but critically as one major
set of accomplishments in the continuing, uncompleted
development of this nation toward full democracy.
This is a development in which more actions, and even
larger ones, are now needed—right away.

6

"The Next and More Profound Stage of the Battle"

President Johnson's stirring speech in June, 1965, was one signal that history had now gone beyond "civil rights," in the narrow sense. He spoke of the importance of equal *"results,"* in addition to equal "rights." In August, 1965, the Watts riot was another and quite different kind of signal that the civil rights laws alone were far from enough: they had not changed the life of millions of poor Negroes in the nation's slums.

Early in the following summer, the nation's mood passed beyond civil rights in still another way. Just five days after the White House Conference "To Fulfill These Rights," James Meredith was shot at while making a walking pilgrimage into Mississippi. During the continuation of the march by many Meredith supporters the nation first heard the term "black power."

These events marked the beginning of a new period —one in which we are still living today. It is a mixed and confusing interim, full of danger—but also of hope. The old days of the civil rights movement, great as they were at their best, are now over. It is a new and different day.

Poverty: the Human Effects of a Twisted History

The first feature of this new situation is a much fuller recognition of the deep remaining consequences of the long *history* of racial discrimination—especially the *economic* consequences. The problem is not just *today's* discrimination and *today's* prejudice (against which the Civil Rights Acts are directed), but the crushing impact of the past. Even if we had eliminated all present-day prejudice and discrimination—which we have not—we would still have this leftover heritage of discrimination-created poverty to deal with.

President Johnson's speech—at the 1965 commencement exercises at Howard University—defined the situation. On the one hand, he said, there is some good news:

"The number of Negroes in schools of higher learning has almost doubled in fifteen years. The number of nonwhite professional workers has more than doubled in ten years. The median income of Negro college women exceeds that of white college women. And there are also the enormous accomplishments of distinguished individual Negroes . . .

"But," the President went on to say, these impressive achievements "tell only the story of a growing middle-class minority. For the great majority of Negro Americans—the poor, the unemployed, the uprooted and the dispossessed—there is a much grimmer story. They are still another nation. Despite the court orders and the laws, despite the legislative victories and the speeches, for them the walls are rising and the gulf widening."

He went on to give statistics, covering the last two or three decades, on the unemployment rate of Negro teen-age boys, on median income of Negroes, on infant mortality of Negroes, and on the number of Negroes living in poverty—all as compared to whites; *in every case the situation for Negroes had become relatively worse.*

"Of course," he said, "Negro Americans as well as white Americans have shared in our rising national abundance." You can then say that Negroes are better off then they once were—and that of course is true. But they are not better off *compared* to the rest of the country—and that is the way we must make the measure.

"First, Negroes are trapped—as many whites are trapped—in inherited, gateless poverty. They lack training and skills. They are shut in slums . . . Private and public poverty combine to cripple their capacities . . .

"There is a second cause—much more difficult to explain, much more deeply grounded, more desperate in its force. It is the devastating heritage of long years of slavery, and a century of oppression, hatred, and injustice.

"For Negro poverty is not white poverty. Many of its causes and many of its cures are the same. But there are differences—deep, corrosive, obstinate differences—radiating painful roots into the community, the family, and the nature of the individual. These differences are not racial differences. They are solely and simply the consequence of ancient brutality, past injustice, and present prejudice . . ."

Other American minorities, said the President, "did

not have a cultural tradition which had been twisted and battered by endless years of hatred and hopelessness."

President Johnson borrowed a figure of speech from Whitney Young, Jr., to indicate the situation that results from this heavy hand of the past: "Freedom is not enough. You do not wipe away the scars of centuries by saying: 'Now you are free to go where you want . . .' You do not take a person who for years has been hobbled by chains and liberate him, bring him to the starting line of a race and then say, 'You are free to compete with all the others,' and still justly believe that you have been completely fair . . . it is not enough just to open the gates of opportunity. All our citizens must have the ability to walk through those gates. This is the next and more profound stage of the battle for civil rights."

President Johnson announced in that speech that he would call a White House Conference on Civil Rights; after some pulling and hauling about its subject matter the conference did gather in Washington a year later, in June of 1966. Massively Negro, it met in two Washington hotels that were segregated when I first came to Washington in 1949.

The theme of the conference was "To Fulfill These Rights," an echo of the title of the report of the Truman civil rights commission almost two decades before, "To Secure These Rights." The conference and its recommendations indicated the new stage of the movement: more than half of the proposals dealt not with racial discrimination but with social and economic disadvantages; they had to do not with Negroes alone, but with all the disadvantaged; though some dealt with

Southern conditions, more dealt with problems of Northern ghettos.

While there was still much to be done in the field of laws against discrimination, the larger work now was clearly elsewhere: in overcoming poverty and eliminating slums.

The success of the first stage of the civil rights movement helped put the spotlight on poverty and the slum as the second stage. As *some* Negroes could now get good jobs, live in good neighborhoods, attend good schools, eat in good restaurants that before were closed to them, it became the more apparent that this meant little to the mass of poor Negroes, left behind in the rural South and inner city. They did not have the money to eat in the restaurants or buy houses in middle-class neighborhoods, and they did not have the education or training to take advantage of new job opportunities. The next stage in the battle for equal opportunity had to be a deliberate attack on the barriers that blocked men from opportunity—barriers not only of race, but of the long history of deprivation: poor schools, poor housing, unemployment and menial jobs, "inherited, gateless poverty"—what I called in my own speech to the White House conference the problem of "slumism."

Here is part of what I said about employment:

I know, and I applaud, the progress which has been made in the past years. Of course, there are countless stories of individual success that would have been impossible a decade ago . . . And I have seen the statistics, and the charts, which demonstrate the rate of progress for Negro Americans in certain job categories, and prove, at least to the man that draws the chart and recites the statistics, that everything is getting better.

But to the unemployed—and often the unemployable— man in Harlem or Woodlawn or Watts, these individual stories of success, and the encouraging statistics, are largely meaningless and sometimes insulting. When the statistical base, that base line, is sufficiently low, any improvement, any increase tends to look better than it actually is. The good news that a Negro has been appointed general counsel of a major corporation brings little hope into the life of a man who failed to complete fifth grade in a second-rate school.

So in all candor 1 will speak within my own criteria, the criteria that I ask you to apply to this conference. We must face honestly the mammoth employment problem which still exists for most Negroes.

Outmoded training programs, tests, recruitment and personnel procedures, apprenticeship requirements, and promotion patterns often deny equal employment achievement as effectively as the old-fashioned "White only—Negroes need not apply" sign that used to hang outside the factory gates.

What I said then still applies, and in other fields, such as education and housing, as well as in employment. Just striking down the old, legally sanctioned discrimination isn't enough; just putting up equal opportunity signs or signing equal opportunity documents isn't enough; just having a token handful of Negro pupils or apprentices or secretaries isn't enough. There has to be "affirmative action" to break down the remaining barriers of custom and inertia and disguised prejudice. There have to be deliberate programs to develop the "ability to walk through those gates." That means an attack on poverty.

In fact, what we have recently done in overcoming poverty is a remarkable achievement—but the frustration and anger of the remaining poor have outdistanced that achievement.

At the end of the decade of the fifties there were nearly forty million Americans in poverty; by the time of the White House conference in 1966 the number had been reduced to about thirty million, and it is lower than that—fewer than twenty-six million—today. The population as a whole has been increasing rather rapidly—adding about two and a half million new Americans each year—so that the reduction in the *percentage* of Americans who live in poverty is striking indeed: from nearly thirty per cent when I came to the Senate in 1949 to about twenty-two per cent in 1959 to fifteen per cent at the time of the conference in 1966 to still less than that in 1968.

We can now say that the American poor have been reduced to less than one-eighth of the nation. And that is measured by our very high American standards. We have come a long way from the day when a great President spoke memorably of the "one-*third* of a nation ill-fed, ill-housed, ill-clothed."

The statistician, the policy-maker, and the civic-minded observer and citizen may rejoice in the great improvement in human happiness these statistics suggest. And historians will say it is an extraordinary accomplishment, probably unmatched—that a nation should by deliberate policy lift these millions of people out of poverty in these few short years.

But all that does not mean much to the man who is still poor. Suppose you are the one American in eight whose children are hungry, whose roof leaks, whose medical care is inadequate, whose schools are inferior —and, worst of all, whose bleak future looks like more of the same. It is cold comfort indeed to tell you then— cheer up, there aren't so many people in your fix as there used to be.

There is a sardonic African proverb: "Full-bellied child says to empty-bellied child, 'Be of good cheer.' "

As we reduce the *proportion* of poverty in this more and more prosperous country, the situation of that remaining smaller fraction becomes more and more difficult.

In the Great Depression we had at least the solace of numbers, of company, of a shared experience. The entire nation was paying attention to our common plight, and trying to find the ways to overcome it. But in the period since World War II we have had a minority poor, a forgotten poor, an "invisible poor" . . . and one-third of it, a black poor.

This has created a difficult political problem, because it is hard to persuade the comfortable majority that the plight of the American poor is real. It is harder still to persuade a *white* majority that they are in part responsible for the condition of the *black* poor.

So despite our wealth and despite our achievements, we now have a hazardous national condition: mounting frustration on the one side, hardening resistance on the other.

The Plight of the City

The problem of race is tangled with the problem of poverty; and now both are mixed with the plight of the city.

Nobody needs to be told today that our cities are in trouble.

One day in July of 1967, after the riots in Newark and Detroit, I said this to some fellow officials of the government in Washington:

> Get in your car and go to Southeast Washington, and then go to Northwest Washington. They are both in the federal city. Take a look. Take a look at the streets. Take a look at the sidewalks. Take a look at the garbage. Why is it that in Northwest Washington you can have receptacles for scrap paper and in Southeast Washington none? Why is it in Northwest Washington the streets can be clean and the sidewalks can be solid and stable, and in Southeast Washington the streets are in havoc? There are people living in both places.

I repeated that a few days later to the mayors and local officials gathered at a meeting, in Boston, of the League of Cities, and I added this:

> You know that in the slums the streets are dirtier than anywhere else in the city, and less frequently swept. And in these areas in the Northern cities the snow is often plowed away the last. The incidence of crime there is the highest; and the vigor of law enforcement there the least. Housing is decrepit, obsolete, broken down . . . If we were as interested in enforcing our building codes as we are in our traffic laws, if you would put out as many tickets on the landlord who refuses to take care of his house as required by the law as you do for the fellow that overparks his car downtown, you'd have a different city.

Part of the problem of the cities is reflected in those quotations: the historic imbalance in municipal services to different sections of the city, the long-time unresponsiveness of some city governments and city agencies to the needs of the slum.

But I don't think that is the root of the problem any more. Today there are many city governments that *want* to respond justly and compassionately to the conditions of the slums—but they lack the resources to do what they would like to do.

As Vice-President I have been the contact man for mayors and city officials in Washington—the liaison between the federal government and city government —and I have held off-the-record seminars on federal-city relations all across the country. The mayors and local officials are struggling with an increasingly unmanageable set of problems. In many cities there has been a transformation in city leadership—but a new set of difficulties, too: the depressing and now familiar list of urban ills. The American city is drastically short of funds, and the pinch is getting worse.

The National Advisory Commission on Civil Disorders—the Kerner Commission—appointed in the aftermath of the riots in 1967, described the "fourfold dilemma" of the American city:

—Fewer tax dollars come in, as large numbers of middle-income taxpayers move out of central cities and property values and business decline;
— more tax dollars are required, to provide essential public services and facilities, and to meet the needs of expanding lower-income groups;
—each tax dollar buys less, because of increasing costs;
—citizen dissatisfaction with municipal services grows as needs, expectations and standards of living increase throughout the community.

In other words, when you look for causes of riots, you have to look at city budgets.

The city and the city's schools have had to depend

primarily upon the property tax—an inequitable and inadequate source of revenue: the more you use it, the more you drive out of the city the industry and the middle-class home-owning citizenry that the city, its schools, its civil life, and its tax base need.

Much of our revenue from federal income and corporation taxes is raised in the cities; much *less* of it comes back to the cities.

A few state governments have tried to do something of what needs to be done for the cities—but the politics of the states, with rural areas and suburbs combining to resist the claims of the cities, makes it very difficult to extract from the state capitols what is needed in the big city halls.

Our tax system is upside down, and getting worse. The gravest needs more and more are in the cities; the resources, more and more, are not in the cities.

I have said that the United States needs a "Marshall Plan for the cities," a program—like the magnificent act following World War II that restored a devastated Europe—that will restore our devastated American cities. I have proposed that the core of such a plan (I spell out the details elsewhere) would be a National Urban Development Bank—a public-private fund to provide money for urban needs, again in the way that we have done abroad.

But meanwhile the cities face mounting problems with dwindling funds—and increasingly they must deal with the whole nation's historic problems of poverty and race. The Kerner Report described the pattern of "white exodus and black migration" which is reshaping our urban centers. "The consequence is a greatly

increased burden on the already depleted resources of
cities, creating a growing crisis of deteriorating facilities and services and unmet human needs.''

The Report tells about the ''formation of the ghetto''
by the Northern migration and the urban migration of
Southern Negroes, and by the rapid increase in the
Negro population.

The relatively higher Negro birth rate makes for a
relatively younger Negro population, and for the high
and rising Negro population in the central city's public schools.

Already proportionately more Negroes live in cities,
and especially big cities, than do whites, and the dis-
proportion is increasing.

The ghetto is caused by population patterns, by the
squeeze on the city, and—the Report said—by ''pervasive segregation and discrimination . . . The ghettos
too often mean men and women without jobs, families
without men, and schools where children are processed
instead of educated, until they return to the street—to
crime, to narcotics, to dependency on welfare, and to
bitterness and resentment against society in general
and white society in particular.''

In the riots that bitterness exploded.

Riots, Justice, and Law

In Watts, 1965; Chicago and Cleveland, 1966; Newark and Detroit, 1967; and in many other cities ''civil
disorders'' defined our new situation in another, terrible way.

On July 27, 1967, just after the devastation in

Newark and Detroit, President Johnson appointed the Kerner Commission. He instructed the eleven-member commission to make a full, fresh, unfettered, nonpartisan study of the riots and of their causes, in depth: "What happened? Why did it happen? What can be done to prevent it from happening again and again? . . . As best you can," said the President, "find the truth and express it in your report."

The composition of the commission was criticized by some people at the time of its appointment for being too "moderate" or conservative—for not including militants, radicals, more black people (there were two Negroes on the commission: Roy Wilkins of the NAACP and Senator Edward Brooke of Massachusetts). But when the commission made its report seven months later, in March of 1968, many of those who had criticized the commission when it was appointed, and who had doubted that it could serve any useful purpose, now welcomed and endorsed it with enthusiasm (and with some surprise).

The commission members heard witnesses, commissioned studies, visited cities themselves—and were shocked by what they saw and heard. To read about the ghetto and about racial violence, or to know about it abstractly, is one thing; to encounter the reality in depth and at first hand is another. The Report concluded that our cities are in a much more serious and dangerous condition than most Americans understand.

Their Report will prove to be a historic document in American life. I fully endorse its recommendations. We must move Congress and the public to act on them. This is not to say that we should shape our human rights program out of fear or panic; we should act, instead, out of a considered conviction about what is just. If we act out of fear, blackmail and extremism are encouraged, and repression wins out in the end. We should go ahead and do what justice has long required of us.

Segregationists and some white conservatives use the riots as an excuse not to take the action for racial justice that they do not support anyway. They are very much afraid we will "reward the rioters," as they say. They focus exclusively on repression if these outbreaks. Ever since Watts, and particularly since Detroit and Newark, the discussion of equal rights has been distorted and sometimes even sidetracked by the very different issues of riots and civil disorders, of "crime in the streets" and "law and order."

Those issues are real. We have to have firm, swift, effective police action against all violent and unlawful behavior. Indeed, lasting progress toward racial and social justice can only occur in a law-abiding and orderly society. But it is a dangerous attitude to substitute that necessary concern for law and order for the equally necessary drive toward racial and social justice. It is dangerous nonsense to believe that social progress and a respect for law are somehow in opposition to each other. The secret of a successfully unfolding constitutional democracy is to have both, complementary to each other, and also reinforcing each other. We respect our law in part because it is responsive to changing social needs; we can make social progress because law and order fasten this progress into the patterns of social life and the habits of the people.

We must condemn and put down looting, arson, and

violent behavior; mob violence and rioting cannot be condoned. The Kerner Report made valuable suggestions for riot control, and we are learning how to put down these civil disorders more effectively. In any case, we have to do it. Order is the first responsibility of government; without it, there can be no justice and no progress. Those who imply that continued rioting and disruption will lead to social progress are very wrong; such behavior leads instead to hardening resistance to progress, and to repression. But we do need insight and understanding as to *why* so much of this reprehensible behavior occurred.

What was the cause of the riots? One trouble with just saying "white racism" is that such an answer may substitute a sweeping collective moralism for social knowledge. The point is not for a whole white "race" to confess its collective sins (it is to be doubted that we should think of collective sins, at least on the part of a "racial" group) but rather for responsible citizens to understand what is happening and to act practically to redirect it.

The first cause of the black ghetto and of the "explosive mixture" that made the riots, the Kerner Report said, is "pervasive discrimination and segregation": "the continuing exclusion of great numbers of Negroes from the benefits of economic progress through discrimination in employment and education, and their enforced confinement in segregated housing and schools." It is against this evil that the civil rights movement—or the first stage of it—was directed. But another cause of the "explosive mixture" in the slums is, ironically, just the "frustrated hope" aroused by civil rights victories: "The expectations aroused by the judicial and legislative victories . . . have led to frustration, hostility." That makes the second stage— of equal results—all the more imperative.

The frustrations of poverty in the midst of very visible and widespread riches are—as I have said —a very important component of the combustible ghetto. We are the first large society in the history of mankind of which it may be said that the *majority* of the people are comfortably fixed. That is a great accomplishment. At the same time, it makes all the more galling the life of that minority of our total population that is left out of the prevailing riches. We appraise our life not by absolute standards but by comparison with those around us; from the misery of Watts, men view the luxury of Beverly Hills. Especially when there seems to be no door from the one to the other, the anger and frustration mount.

And now we have in the TV set an instrument that emphasizes the contrast. As the Kerner group said: "Through television—the universal appliance in the ghetto—and the other media of mass communications, this affluence has been endlessly flaunted before the eyes of the Negro poor and the jobless ghetto youth."

The "inherited, gateless poverty" of the black ghetto exists in the midst of tantalizing, widespread, but unattainable riches and luxury. Discrimination— past and present —seems to have locked out the poor urban Negro—locked him out of the possibilities of American life. There is a deep feeling of powerlessness—of inability to change these conditions. And then comes the atmosphere of violence (white terrorism, black ex-

tremism) and some spark—usually a trivial incident
involving the police—and then there is a riot.

"Militants" tended to endorse the way the Report
placed the blame on "white racism," while conservatives and some moderates, in varying degrees, criticized that point. The point is not to be "militant" or
radical, or liberal, or conservative, or "moderate,"
but to be accurate. The accurate point is that our society has built into it from the past a structure of
racial inequality. The sound objective is a rebuilt
society from which that inequality has been eliminated.

This subject—as I have had plenty of opportunity to
learn—is full of moralizing, of emotion, of recrimina-
tion, guilt, and ideological one-upmanship. I think one
has to keep one's eye steadily on the destination
through a great deal of ideological storm-tossing. The
destination is a multi-racial society of equals. In the
effort to get there, one must appeal to the conscience
of white America, and condemn the immorality of
racial prejudice in a man's heart and of racial inequality in society. But one must also accompany one's
moral appeals and moral condemnations with planned
practical action for social change, based on social
knowledge.

We are not going to rebuild a society and accomplish
full equality by dramatic conversions of whites (valuable though these are) or even by mass conversion
(which is rather unlikely) but rather by deliberate and
specific social change.

To the moralistic and militant, one may say this: It
is all very well to demand justice now and absolutely

to condemn the immorality of white racism. At the same time you have to look at what is happening in society, and to devise the specific programs to serve the purposes of justice. And you have to find the way to enact these programs.

To the complacent and conservative, one may say this: It is all very well to insist on law and order, and to say that the rioters themselves must be condemned. At the same time you have to look at what gives rise to the riots. They explode out of real social conditions that you can't ignore. You have to do far more than just "support your local police"; you also have to support concrete programs to change the social conditions that are now giving your local police such a difficult job.

The Crisis of Optimism

Expectations inevitably rise faster than fulfillment. And progress itself arouses fervor against the remaining barriers. In commenting on the black today, many of us have quoted de Toqueville:

> The sufferings that are endured patiently, as being inevitable, become intolerable the moment that it appears that there might be an escape. Reform then only serves to reveal more clearly what still remains oppressive and now all the more unbearable; the suffering, it is true, has been reduced, but one's sensitivity has become more acute.

What we are experiencing—bad as it is some ways, and dangerous to the nation—is the agony of progress. We must diminish the agony and turmoil—but to do that, we must accelerate the progress.

The distinguished novelist Ralph Ellison, one of the wisest of American writers, defined our present and future situation in a remarkable way two years ago, at the Senate hearings on urban problems chaired by Senator Ribicoff. Mr. Ellison made his observations in response to questions by the late Senator Robert Kennedy, in a very interesting exchange.

Senator Kennedy: What is it, Mr. Ellison, do you anticipate will be the relationships of the whites and the Negroes in this country, particularly in our urban centers over the period of the next decade?

Mr. Ellison: If we have luck, Senator, proper things will be put in their proper places. A share of the responsibility for ruling, or analyzing, the conditions which mar the city—and I am not just speaking of Negro slums, but of the whole city—will be assumed by Negroes. We will be able to seek out and develop those leaders who through military experience, who through experience in the arts, who through some other forms of experience have acquired some vital knowledge and skills to offer to the city as a whole.

Senator Kennedy: What is the alternative to that?

Mr. Ellison: The alternative to that will be an increase among those Negroes who feel hopeless at the very time when things seem to be changing. I think we have to recognize that the political acts which have brought Negroes the promise of more freedom by terminating ninety years and more of political practice and social custom have by the very fact of termination created a degree of chaos. We have decreed the new but the conditions under which the new can emerge have not been created.

Senator Kennedy: Yes.

Mr. Ellison: That is because the legislation is in many instances far ahead of the political structures which exist. People don't know quite how to use this new freedom, this new possibility of democracy. We have got to learn that.

But as we learn it, I think we have to be aware that there is a crisis of optimism among Negroes. Slavery couldn't bring this crisis about. Depressions nor wars did not bring it about. But now, in the Northern cities, there is a crisis because things don't appear to be happening fast enough. . . . Much money has been allocated, but it takes more money to get the allocations to the people. This isn't understood by a lot of Negroes who are far away from any large sums of money . . .

Mr. Ellison then went on to indicate the particular importance of the Negro's faith in America:

. . . We have to be aware that if the American Negro loses his optimistic attitude toward the American promise, the whole nation is in trouble. Because we have been, ironically, one of the main supports of American optimism. As long as we Negroes believed in the possibilities of making order out of this chaos of diversified races and religions and regions, everybody could have faith. But if the Negro loses his optimism, then suddenly the supports will have been lost, for the man at the bottom will no longer believe in the burden of possibility.

Senator Kennedy then asked Ralph Ellison where we are headed; and in Mr. Ellison's answer, there is an interesting reference to the role of the South:

Senator Kennedy: Would you agree that we are at the moment on sort of a razor's edge in the direction that we are going ultimately to be headed, as to whether we are going to fall off into this chasm of lack of hope versus the other side which gives us some opportunity for the future?

Mr. Ellison: Well, I must remain optimistic. I must remain optimistic because fortunately, as we reach crises in the cities of the North, there is a parallel expansion of freedom for Negroes in the South. And as the next two generations, say, of college people leave the North and go

South, or others remain to find places within the South—and this is very important—and as they start functioning within the governments of the South, the Negro in the Northern slum is going to feel much more optimistic about his own chances. Perhaps the South is where he is going to have to look for hope, just as the nation is going to have to look to the new South for instruction. For it might well be that the place where all the trouble started will be the place where we will begin to see the most immediate effects of the change which has been set in motion.

The New Racial Consciousness

Finally, our situation now is marked by a new kind of emphasis on color and on race, now especially by "black" (as we are learning to say) Americans proudly, searchingly, sometimes in despair and sometimes in defiance, seeking a new role and identity.

In the old days of the civil rights movement we sought to *ignore* race and color, and to treat each man, as we used to say, as an *individual*; we wanted the benefits of this society available to all persons—in the familiar phrase of American speechmaking—"without regard to race, creed, or color." That is still what we seek in the long run. But in the short run, now, in this new situation, we have learned that we have to pay attention to race and color.

In social policy, where "anti-discrimination" laws alone are not enough, "affirmative action" must take account of race. We must count the numbers of black students or Negro apprentices or minority group members who are advanced—otherwise there is little or no change.

And in our social life, too, we have learned that we

have to pay attention to race, and to emphasize color,
favorably—in order to overcome the *past* emphasis,
which was unfavorable. We can't just wave a wand and
say we will see all men as equals without paying any
attention to race—when for centuries our culture *has*
paid attention to it. We have a terrible black-white
theme in our society.

We Americans are all caught in a tragic and tangled
web of racial history.

A Negro child comes home one sad day, hurt and
bewildered, and asks his parents: "What makes white
folks so mean?" A Negro novelist cries out that he is
"invisible," that his fellow citizens don't even see *him*
as a man. Many condemn the whole society as "racist,"
and a black militant says "whitey" is a devil.

An ordinary white American, on the other hand, is
confused and hurt by all this. He doesn't feel that he
has any racial prejudices, or any hatred in him. He
tries to justify himself by telling about his Negro
co-workers, Negro children at his children's birthday
parties—and then is hurt all the more when this is
brusquely rejected and seems even to make things
worse. If he is a "white liberal" he may cite what he
has done for civil rights and brotherhood—and be
chagrined when that is brushed aside. Other white
Americans may turn belligerent and nasty.

When the Kerner Report said "white racism" was
the root of our racial turmoil, many Negroes and many
white radicals and liberals applauded. At last, they
said, an official government document put the blame
squarely where it belongs. But many other white citizens firmly rejected that idea. They felt no guilt; they

denied that they personally were "racists"; they repudiated the notion that the whole society is racist.

I think it is important, in order to achieve both equality and reconciliation, that we try to sort out the truth of this matter. We need to understand how deeply racial inequality is built into the themes of our culture and the institutions of our society. It has been built into our American life by the terrible history of slavery, segregation, and discrimination. A white person in America, consciously or unconsciously, assumes his superiority just by skin color; a black person has been taught to assume his inferiority. In Dr. Kenneth Clark's famous experiments, the little black girl, asked to pick the doll that looked like herself, kept rejecting the brown doll; Negro children, asked to crayon a figure in a coloring book the shade they were, would color it purple, or scratch across it— emotionally rejecting their own skin tone. A mother comes home to find her six-year-old crying in the bathroom, scrubbing himself, trying to wash off his brown skin. We need a determined, unrelenting campaign against this terrible nonsense in our culture. And the black power movement is right to try to correct its effect on black citizens: there should be a new Negro history, black consciousness, black pride.

But that is not to heap guilt on the "white" man as such. One can understand how a proud man like the late Malcolm X, experiencing brutal mistreatment and learning about slavery, should conclude that the "white" man is, categorically, a "devil." But different "white" men behave differently. If we must understand how a ghetto Negro is caught in his environment,

shaped by it, so, too, we must understand the same of
the ordinary resistant white man. If we should think
of the black man as simply a white man with a black
skin (as in the end we should), so we should also do
the reverse: so-called "white" men are nothing worse
(or better) than what black men would be had they
"white" skins.

In other words, we are all men. Despite all the differences culture forces onto people because of color, still
the physical difference of so-called races has no fundamental or eternal significance whatever. Malcolm X,
after experiences in other cultures, was beginning to
figure that out at the end of his life.

In his remarkable autobiography Malcolm X tells
about a full afternoon's conversation he had in 1965
with a white ambassador to an African country, who,
he says, was "Africa's most respected American ambassador."

Based on what I had heard of him I had to believe him
when he told me that as long as he was on the African continent, he never thought in terms of race, that he dealt with
human beings, never noticing their color. He said he was
more aware of language differences than of color differences. He said that only when he returned to America
would he become aware of color differences.

I told him, "What you are telling me is that it isn't the
American white *man* who is a racist, but it's the American
political, economic, and social *atmosphere* that automatically nourishes a racist psychology in the white man." He
agreed.

We both agreed that American society makes it next to
impossible for humans to meet in America and not be conscious of color differences. And we both agreed that if

racism could be removed, America could offer a society where rich and poor could truly live like human beings.

That discussion with the ambassador gave me a new insight—one which I like: that the white man is *not* inherently evil, but America's racist society influences him to act evilly. The society has produced and nourishes a psychology which brings out the lowest, most base part of human beings.

I don't agree with that last sentence, but the insight that Malcolm X was beginning to work out seems to me close to the heart of the matter: not white racial guilt, white racial evil, but a culture and society distorted and damaged by history on the matter of race. That distortion and damage are present in the American society, affecting all of us (Negroes, too), whether or not we individually share in its worst expressions. We participate passively, at least, in the pattern that oppresses the American Negro.

Some day—hopefully soon—we really will be able to drop all the nonsense about race, and deal with each other just as equals and as persons. But first we have some bad history to overcome.

7

A Program
for Participation

Historians will regard the period from the assassination of John Kennedy in November, 1963, to the election of a conservative Congress in November, 1966, as one of the most productive in American history. We enacted the greater part of the social legislation for which we had been fighting since World War II, plus a lot more that had only recently been thought of.

The first bill I introduced in 1949, when I came to the Senate, was a Medicare bill—and in 1965 we finally enacted one. All through the years that I was in the Senate we fought for federal aid to education, to give help to our schools; year after year we were beaten, by one complication or another—usually the "religious issue." Finally in 1965 we won that one, too, and in a significant way: by ticketing the biggest part of the federal money for the schools in areas of poverty.

There was a great excitement in Washington in those years; much that we were doing had been stored up from the past, but a lot of it was news, too. President Johnson's anonymous task forces of 1964 came up with an extraordinary set of new ideas: Project Headstart and rent supplements and model cities and the Teacher Corps and many more.

These were enacted into law in a period unmatched in accomplishment, at least since the height of the New Deal.

But—as I have said—much poverty remained, more visible now that we had proclaimed "war" against it, and more galling now that so many more Americans were prosperious. And a large fraction of the poor was black, their lives unchanged by the civil rights laws or our poverty programs.

First we had the actions for civil rights that I have described.

Then more people began to see that they weren't enough.

We needed not only *fair* employment but also *full* employment—training, income, and jobs for the poor.

We needed not only *integrated* education but also a *good* education—money, good teachers, remedial reading, small classes for the schools in the central cities.

We needed not only *fair* housing but also *enough* housing—standard housing, "decent, safe, and sanitary" housing—for all. There had to be full employment and full education, and "a decent home in a suitable living environment for every American family."

There is still this separate country of poverty, a shrinking yet still large fraction of the American population (more numerous, in fact, than most of the nations on the globe), that is more or less shut out of the material benefits and opportunities of American democracy. One-third are Negro, barred from full participation both by a heritage of poverty and by racial discrimination.

The first priority, in this "next and more profound stage" of the equal rights movement, is to bring forward into American society these people who have been left behind for so long a time.

I can't give the details of policy proposals here; there isn't space, and this book isn't the place. But I can suggest a guideline or two.

A program for equality must now become a program for *participation*.

It must be a deliberate, sensitive, planned program to allow people to come in—to help them attain the ability to walk through those gates of opportunity.

It must be a program not of the federal government alone, but also of states and cities; not of government alone, but of the private sector and voluntary associations, too, working together—"creative federalism."

It must be a program not of handouts or of charity, but of opening new opportunities for self-help and dignity.

It must enable citizens to participate in politics, in a broad range of social institutions, and above all—in the American economy.

Jobs for All; a Decent Welfare System

Of course, that is the foundation: a job, an income.

Nothing stands in the way today of our eliminating poverty in this country except our decision as a nation to *do* it.

We have the resources. It costs us more as a nation today—in welfare payments, unemployment insurance, the price of disease, and of crime traceable to poverty

—to permit poverty to continue than it would cost to put to work every person willing and able to work.

There is poverty in this country today only because we do not yet fully sense the change that has taken place. Poverty is now an inhuman anachronism.

The first answer to poverty is full employment—the opportunity for all to work. The poor—like everyone else—really prefer to work, to have a job, to do meaningful and respected activity. A man needs a job to have self-respect and the respect of his fellows—and he needs respect, most of all, so that we no longer have "two nations," one of them poor, isolated, and regarded with hostility.

And it is a disgrace to our humanity that as I write this there is still severe malnutrition, there are hungry children, even starving people, in this lush, rich country. Henceforth, if I may put it this way, it should be against the law to starve to death in the United States.

There must be a program, supplanting the old grudging and inadequate welfare system, that will support the income of all people in need, so that they can live in dignity.

We have learned a lot from our earnest efforts in the war on poverty. I think mainly we have learned this: a new basic welfare system, the foundation of a program against poverty, ought to be national and universally applicable, not selectively given out here and there. It should cover *everybody* in need—whatever his race, wherever he lives, whether he is a part of some organization or not (lots of the direst poverty in the land is still hidden away, silent and unnoticed in the country's corners). It should not require clamor, conflict, scrambling for funds. It ought to function like the social security system—automatically, for all. It ought to treat people with dignity, not make them dependent or importunate or resentful. It should free welfare workers to help and heal, instead of making them investigate, snoop, and report. A decent life, in this wealthy country, should now be considered a *right* for all men—which ties in, too, with human dignity. What a man receives in this country is his by right, not by charity or clamor, and is rightly claimed by all.

At the same time, then, there should be an end to irrational expectations, built out of the vagueness of our promises. One of our troubles is that expectations often run far beyond what realistically we can do. It is cruel to any man, and especially to a poor man, to arouse hopes that are not fulfilled. But let's plan carefully what we can do—and do it.

The Kerner Report quoted the welfare commissioner of New York City as saying this, about our present "welfare" system: "The welfare system is designed to save money instead of people and tragically ends by doing neither." Its complicated labyrinthine method gives aid by categories only (blind, handicapped, dependent children) and leaves out many who are equally in need. It varies enormously among states, which is inequitable and has bad social effects—encouraging people to leave Southern states for the illusory gains of the Northern cities. The rates are too low, leaving people on welfare in many states still below the government's own poverty line (thus we keep people in the poverty we say we are fighting). It often encourages dependency and discourages initiative. Let's do it right.

In the long run that will cost less not more, making more people tax-paying, self-respecting citizens and consumers instead of tax-eating dependents.

That means, too—another basic principle—that there has to be an incentive system: supplementary benefits and allowable income to improve one's situation. The present welfare system sometimes actually penalizes people for earning money. That's because we are so grudging and frightened about it, so terribly afraid that some "lazy bum" is going to take advantage of us. Surely we don't need to be nasty and suspicious about it—most of those we are talking about are dependent children. By our grudging fears we make the system more costly as well as inhumane. Let's stop all that and do it right.

Room at the Top for Black People

A job for all who can work and a decent welfare system form the foundation for a program for participation- -but just the foundation. The building itself requires far more: upgrading, promotion, a chance to get ahead, access to capital, an opportunity for higher education—in short, full participation in America's dream: that any man can make his way, as far as he can go, by his own effort and talent. For much of white America (not by any means all of it) that dream has come true; for much of black America it has been at best a "dream deferred," more often a cruel illusion.

White Americans often overestimate the position of Negro Americans, and judge from a few isolated examples. Look at the statistics. As I said, on May 2,

1968, in Philadelphia: "Count forty white Americans. One is a proprietor. To find one black proprietor, count one thousand. And with rare exceptions, he is in a marginal business . . ." Typically, he runs a barbershop, a funeral parlor, a small grocery store, or other small retail or service business.

There are 31,000 auto dealerships in the United States; how many of them are owned by Negroes? A grand total of *six* today—until very recently, just *one*.

Typically, one major U.S. manufacturing company has 8,000 subcontractors—not one of them Negro-owned.

Negroes make up twelve percent of our population, but own less than one percent of American businesses. Less than three percent of "self-employed" Americans are non-white. Only three and a half percent of the non-white in the U.S. labor force are managers, officials, or proprietors—compared to fourteen and a half percent of whites.

A new "educational minimum wage," a new chance for all able students to go to college, the existing anti-discrimination laws, and a new spirit in our voluntary associations will open the professions more fully to Negroes. As we correct the unfair treatment of Negroes, especially in our education system, we can expect more of them to become scholars, teachers, doctors, scientists, lawyers, public administrators, and educational administrators (there is special need right now for these last two). There will be Negroes in the downtown law firms, Negro bank presidents, more Negro professors in top universities, more Negro scientists and engineers and scholars.

What about the business world?

In the aftermath of the Watts riot in August, 1965, I met with industrial leaders in Los Angeles to see what we could do about the severe unemployment in Watts. The Aero-Jet General Corporation decided to establish a firm in the heart of Watts, a firm that would hire residents and train them *on the job*. When the Areo-Jet subsidiary started two years ago its founders set as their goal for mid-1968 a work force of 100 employees and sales of two and a half million dollars. Watts Manufacturing has exceeded those goals. It has 500 employees and expects by this year's end to achieve sales of four and a half to five million dollars.

On January 29, 1968, as Vice-President, I asked that representatives of five federal agencies meet with me to consider the subject of "minority entrepreneurship." I said in my memorandum:

> I am convinced that there is a great economic and social potential, often not recognized, in enlarging opportunities for members of minority groups as entrepreneurs. At present, Negroes and Spanish-speaking groups own or control only a minute portion of the business in this country. The businesses they do operate are usually small and uneconomic. *The urgent need is to have minority groups own and run more substantial businesses which are fully competitive in the American economy.*

We then held a series of meetings of top officials of government departments, and from their report I developed some conclusions and a program. Black entrepreneurs need what any entrepreneurs need—working capital, training and know-how, and markets—but the heritage of racial discrimination has made it hard for the aspiring Negro businessman to obtain them. I have proposed in detailed reports a full new program of assistance to inner-city businessmen, to help provide access to each of the needed elements. We have to recognize that solid public assistance is necessary because racial inequality and poverty have effectively shut out most of black America from the centers of American business and finance (it is deceptive to talk about "black capitalism" and not propose realistic support to make it come about). We also have to be sure that the necessary assistance is provided without impairing the initiative and responsibility of black business and inner-city communities.

There has been a kind of unspoken, unrecognized conspiracy in white America that has kept Negro Americans out of the upper and middle ranks of the American system of business and the professions. We now have to act deliberately and specifically to correct the pattern created by the barriers of the past.

Citizen Participation

Negro Americans must be allowed to participate fully in the American economic system—and in the political system, too. I have made some remarks already about the franchise and about Negro leaders in government. I think there is another point to be made, about citizen participation in a broader sense.

I think we all have learned now about the importance of the poor, and disinherited, and black acting for themselves.

It may be true that we liberals have sometimes

seemed to think of ourselves as nobly bestowing benefits on the "less fortunate." It may be that some
seemed to expect credit or gratitude for their bene-
ficence. If so, the social action of the sixties has effectively ended that.

The poor, the Negro, the slum-dweller, the "forgotten people" are gaining a new self-confidence. With
young idealists and new leaders they are not only de-
manding the social and economic benefits that we liberals have historically fought for; they are also de-
manding full participation. They insist on the right to
have their say in the decisions that affect their lives.

The civil rights workers in the rural South learned
how important it is for people who have been rejected
and oppressed to have a movement they can call their
own. Bread and food stamps and jobs and pre-kinder-
garten schooling and equal treatment at the lunch
counter are all very important. But the self-respect that
comes from voting, speaking, participating—in other
words, from self-government, from democracy—is even
more important.

The residents of the ghettos insist that our urban
renewal projects, our "model cities" planning, *must*
take account of the desires of the people who live in the
neighborhood. They are right to insist; planning must
be done by and with the people, not just *for* the people.

Leaders of the poor have seized upon the phrase in
the Economic Opportunity Act of 1964 that calls for
"maximum feasible participation of the residents of
the areas served"; they insist that the poor themselves
have a place on the boards of our anti-poverty projects.

All we are doing and propose to do will fall short

until there is a full sharing—black and white, "majority groups" and "minority groups"—of participation and responsibility.

The programs that show the greatest promise are those that permit the largest possible participation and responsibility on the part of those who are principally involved.

The Negro community should have and should take a far larger part than it has up to now in the operation of the necessary machinery of law and order. There is much more than amusement in the recent proposal of one civil rights organization to start an "Adopt a Cop" program.

I think the community councils we set up in Minneapolis after 1945 were a forerunner of what is good in today's "participatory democracy." We didn't call it by that name, but the idea was similar. When I became Mayor we broke up the city into thirteen neighborhoods, with a community council for each. We decentralized city government that way. These community councils advised on recreation, public health, sanitation, traffic, and public works—and all the rest of the municipal services in their area, including the police. I think more cities today could use community councils like those.

And then you could say the idea of community participation goes back a lot farther than that. Some of the current proponents might not like to hear it put this way, but the idea goes back to the very essence of an older liberalism. Liberalism historically sought the broadening of the franchise toward universal suffrage. Successive movements of American liberalism—Jeffersonian, Jacksonian, Abolitionist, Populist, Rooseveltian

—each brought new voices, new groups into our democratic politics: the man without property, the common man, the farmer, the ex-slave, the Westerner, the immigrant. And now the social revolution of the sixties is doing that once more.

There is an enormous gulf between the impoverished, largely Negro, masses of the inner city and the rural South, on the one hand, and most of the rest of the society, on the other. We have underestimated that gulf. We did not fully appreciate the cultural shock of a mistreated, uneducated Alabama tenant farmer's suddenly encountering the confusion and hostility of Chicago, the complexity of Harlem and Watts.

We need to find the ways not only to bring jobs and better education to these citizens, but also to allow them to speak and act and participate in government.

The minority that lives in a separated culture of poverty, surrounded by a vast majority culture of plenty, may need a megaphone to make itself heard.

But still—it does not need a club.

It does not need, and cannot gain from, dogmatic, quasi-Marxist philosophies of necessary conflict, wholesale alienation, contemptuous and cynical attack upon the community, antagonizing all the other parts of it.

It cannot be helped by deliberately polarizing the institutions of our society,

One conviction of American democracy is that people must speak for themselves, choose their own way; it must not have leaders, programs, or policies imposed upon them from "outside," by people who do not understand, by people with whom they do not identify.

But another conviction of American democracy is

this: that the voice of the disinherited *can* be heard, and social justice *can* be attained, *within* the institutions of American society: within the framework of the rule of law, of the Constitution, of consensus and democratic practice.

Freedom to Choose a Home

The black, the poor, the excluded must now be fully allowed into our economic system and into our political system (in the broadest sense). And they must also have freedom to choose where their home will be. To participate fully in the benefits of this democratic society, you have to be allowed freedom in this basic decision: where you will live.

Although many white Americans don't like to let themselves admit it, that obviously has been a problem for black Americans.

Let me quote again from the Kerner Report, on the different pattern for Negroes: most of them could not follow the "old tenement trail," up and out of the ghetto, which other ethnic groups followed:

> As the whites were absorbed by the larger society many left their predominantly ethnic neighborhoods and moved to outlying areas . . . Nowhere has the expansion of America's urban Negro population followed this pattern of dispersal. Thousands of Negro families have attained incomes, living standards, and cultural levels matching or surpassing those of whites who have "upgraded" themselves from distinctively ethnic neighborhoods. Yet most Negro families have remained within predominantly Negro neighborhoods, primarily because they have been effectively excluded from white residential areas.

Their exclusion has been accomplished through various discriminatory practices, some obvious and overt, others subtle and hidden. Deliberate efforts are sometimes made to discourage Negro families from purchasing or renting homes in all-white neighborhoods. Intimidation and threats of violence have ranged from throwing garbage on lawns and making threatening phone calls to burning crosses in yards and even dynamiting property. More often, real estate agents simply refuse to show homes to Negro buyers.

Many middle-class Negro families, therefore, cease looking for homes beyond all-Negro areas or nearby "changing" neighborhoods. For them, trying to move into all-white neighborhoods is not worth the psychological effort and costs required.

In another place the Report summarized this point: "The past pattern of white ethnic groups gradually moving out of central city areas to middle-class suburbs has not applied to Negroes. Effective open housing laws will help make this possible . . ."

In its recommendations the Kerner Commission endorsed a "national, comprehensive, and enforceable open-occupancy law. . . .

"We have canvassed the various alternatives and have come to the firm opinion that there is no substitute for enactment of a federal fair housing law. The key to breaking down housing discrimination is universal and uniform coverage, and such coverage is attainable only through federal legislation. . . .

"We urge that such a statute be enacted at the earliest possible date."

Members of the Commission publicly urged Congress to enact the open housing provision in the administration's civil rights bill, introduced in the Senate by my friend and successor as Senator from Minnesota, Walter Mondale.

But the truth is that open housing had not been the most popular issue with the American voter. In 1964 voters in California overwhelmingly passed "Proposition 14"—against fair housing legislation—by more than two to one, and politicians everywhere could see what that meant. Milwaukee's angry confrontations and marches had had to do chiefly with a proposed open housing ordinance. In the past, voters in city after city had voted down open housing.

President Kennedy, largely for reasons of congressional politics, had delayed taking executive action on housing until late 1962. Then, by a "stroke of the pen," he did sign an executive order that required antidiscrimination pledges thereafter (but not retroactively) for federally assisted housing. The order had a disappointingly minimal effect.

Open housing thus was the one large field still left to be dealt with by federal law after the comprehensive Civil Rights Acts of 1964 and 1965. The civil rights bill proposed by the Johnson administration in 1966 featured an open housing section—but it died under the threat of a filibuster. There wasn't much public support for the bill. In marked contrast to the tremendous public attention and effective lobbying by a broad coalition in 1964 and 1965, one participant said you could have put all the people working for the passage of the civil rights bill in 1966 into one elevator.

The prospects did not look much better for an open housing section in the 1967–68 Congress, although we argued strongly for it. Senators Mondale and Brooke sponsored the kind of universal open occupancy the Kerner Commission was later to recommend.

The administration faced the question whether to include a strong plug for the open housing bill in the State of the Union message and the administration's program. The question was whether we had any chance at all to see it pass. I argued that we should go for broke.

The Senate took up the bill at the start of the second session, in January, 1968, after the shock of the 1967 summer riots. After the debate had gone on for a few weeks, I saw Senator Dirksen at a White House dinner for Prime Minister Harold Wilson. He came up to me and put his arm around me and said: "Well, I guess we should have you back up there. [He meant in the Senate.] You and I could work it out. We've got to get a bill. I know we could work it out. I wish you were there."

I said: "Well, Everett, I'll try to stop by to see you."

He said: "I wish you would."

I told the President about my conversation with Senator Dirksen, and then the next day I called Attorney General Ramsey Clark, who was working on the bill, and told him what Senator Dirksen had said. In the meantime he, too, had talked to Senator Dirksen. "I think Everett is in a more favorable mood," he said. "I was really surprised at how he had had a change of heart."

Then I got on the phone and called Senator Dirksen. This was on Friday, after the Wilson dinner on Thursday. Mr. Dirksen wasn't feeling well, so we had a conversation for about forty-five minutes on the phone. It was 1964 all over again. We reminisced, and then I said: "Everett, I'm going to lay it on the line. Without you there won't be any civil rights bill. It's exactly where we were in 1964. That year we laid the foundation. Now let's finish the edifice we started then."

The next morning Senator Dirksen called Ramsey Clark and said: "Come on over. I want to go to work."

Suddenly it looked as though there could be a bill after all. Senator Dirksen changed his position, and said he would support closure and a fair housing provision. The civil rights Senators were jubilant. They were quite willing to make the compromises Senator Dirksen requested—the elimination from coverage of a fraction of single-family housing—in return for his support for closure on a bill with fair housing still in it.

But then it appeared that Senator Dirksen might not have his troops. Three times the effort to enact closure on this bill failed, and the fourth time, Majority Leader Mansfield announced, would have to be the last. If closure failed again, the bill would be dead.

I saw Senator Dirksen again before this vote and asked him how things were coming. He said they didn't look too good. I said: "Everett, you know you've just got to take control of the boys that work with you. We'll take control of ours. Phil will work with you [Senator Philip Hart of Michigan, floor leader on the bill] and we will get closure." On the weekend before the fourth—final—vote on closure I called him again and said: "Everett, we just can't have defeat when we are within two or three votes. You've got to get a couple, and I'll get a couple." We talked about a Republican Senator from the Midwest who likes to be sure his amendments are considered, and I said to tell that Senator the Vice-President would be helpful with those amendments.

That closure vote came on Monday, March 2; on Sunday, the day before, the Kerner Commission had released its report.

I was presiding in the Senate (I have thus been in the Senate all three times in history that closure has been voted on a civil rights bill, once as floor leader of the bill and twice as presiding officer). Although nothing for me will match the excitement of the 1964 vote, the 1968 vote had its own drama; closure was voted by the slimmest possible margin, without a single vote to spare (65 to 32 with three absent— just barely two-thirds of those voting), and three of the Senators whose votes were in doubt and who switched to make closure possible cast their votes after the roll call had been completed and it appeared that we had lost. When Senator Cannon came through the door, and signaled to me in the chair with a victory circle made by his thumb and forefinger, I knew that we would make it. And—just barely—we did.

Then, ironically, the problem was the House of Representatives. In 1966, as in many previous years, the House had passed a civil rights bill that the Senate killed. This one had an open housing provision; it was defeated by the threat of filibuster in the Senate. Now in 1968 we had broken through the filibuster and passed a strong bill in the Senate—only to see it in danger in the House.

The House had become more conservative, and it

strongly reflected suburban anxieties about Negroes. We in the administration pressed for quick action by the House on the Senate bill to pass the bill before the Easter recess, and to obviate a conference and a long battle during which the opposing forces could mobilize. But House Republican leader Gerald Ford opposed the idea, and it appeared that the struggle might go on through the spring.

Then on the night of April 4 we got the news that Martin Luther King, Jr., had been murdered. We held meetings at the White House all the next day, and one of the first things we hoped could be done, in the aftermath of this terrible deed, was the passage by the House of the civil rights bill. The President strongly urged the House to act.

There were riots in Washington on that Friday and on the weekend, with the ugly sight of black smoke over the White House, a machine gun guarding the Capitol, and troops in the streets. Some Congressmen reacted with angry vituperation. To their credit, however, most were able to separate the question of the civil rights bill from the question of the riots.

On April 10, the day after King's funeral, with troops still guarding the Capitol, the House passed the Civil Rights Act of 1968. The President quickly signed it into law.

Now fair housing is the law of the land. Eighty percent of the nation's housing will be covered by it— everything except the sale by the owner, without a real estate broker, of a single-family house, and multiple-unit developments and apartments of fewer than four units. Many were surprised that we were able to pass so strong an act.

Nine weeks later there was another surprise: the Supreme Court ruled that the Civil Rights Act of *1866* is the law of the land, and prohibited *all* discrimination in housing, right now. Nobody can discriminate; no housing is exempt; *all* racial discrimination in housing is now illegal in the United States.

The problem now is to see that the laws are enforced. And this is a particularly difficult field for enforcement.

Many of the best real estate men have now come around to genuine support not only for the law but for the principle of open occupancy. Even before the law passed, it was announced that from now on all Levitt developments—North and South—would be open to all without regard to race. In the year preceding these national actions as many municipal open housing laws had been passed as in all previous years put together. After the federal law was written the Milwaukee city council, which had adamantly resisted an ordinance through a long and angry history of marches, riots, and controversy, now quickly enacted an ordinance going beyond the federal law.

Some black leaders place little emphasis on open occupancy, because they don't want Negroes to move out of the ghetto to suburbs and white sections of town; instead they want to build the black political power of numbers in the ghetto. I answer: nobody should tell an individual where he cannot live, on racial grounds, whether white real estate agents, white suburbanites— or black power leaders.

Ghetto Enrichment Plus Integration

My position on the current phase of the struggle is in agreement with the National Advisory Commission on Civil Disorders.

What did the Commission say?

They said that our "present policies" are far from adequate—they won't bring justice, and they won't bring peace.

They said that new ghetto "enrichment" policies that would pour new funds and bring new business into the ghetto, and recognize indigenous "black" leaders and organizations, though necessary, are not enough. They said they should be treated as interim policies, not permanent ones.

The Commission recommended instead a policy of "enrichment—*plus* integration"—and so do I.

We do need the "enrichment" of the inner city because—whether we like it or not—the ghetto is still going to be there for some years. A generation will grow up in those schools, live in those houses, dodge the dangers of those streets, deal with those institutions, face the prospects of employment available—or not available—in those sections of town. It is not realistic to expect much integration—for example—in the public schools of Washington, D.C., already over eighty percent non-white. Many other city school systems—as the Kerner Report indicated—are coming to be like that, too. For those schools, for the immediate future, smaller classes, remedial reading teachers, *quality* education are primary answers.

The inner-city Negro sections are going to be the

home of millions of Americans for a number of years. We have to open opportunities *there* and *now*—not someplace else, later.

And the black power advocates, as I have said, make some important points, too:

Group pride is essential, especially for a people long oppressed and humiliated.

A chance to have black leaders and black organization is of great importance to a people long taught to have a negative self-image.

Some control, some power, some real participation in decisions are necessary for people who have long felt themselves to be powerless and dependent.

The people of the ghetto must have their own thing. They must be given a chance to stand on their own feet and make their own way.

The old pattern of dependence and subservience must be stopped (in the welfare system, for example, and in too many schools, too many housing projects, and— yes—too many sections of political parties, including my own).

The Kerner Report calls all this "enrichment," because it requires that lots of new money be put into inner-city institutions. And it does. It is important that we recognize that. Some whites resist it, some blacks have slurred it over—but there is no way around that fact. A much greater part of the nation's resources must be put into the desperately needy, blighted, and bitter centers of our nation's cities—money for health, not money for sickness.

We put in lots of money there now—in the inadequate but costly welfare system, in guarding against, and rebuilding after, riots. Smaller class sizes, better-paid teachers, decent housing—those things will take money, too—and it will be money spent in a far better way. But money isn't enough. It has to be money without domination. It has to be a help to the neighborhood's own life and growth—not a "welfare colonialism" that stamps it out.

"Enrichment" is the Report's word. I would call it this—Neighborhood Strength.

New life in the ghetto neighborhood is good, and necessary, and realistic. It is realistic, if you look at the population figures for our cities. It is realistic, if you hear the proud cry of independence of young black Americans. But it isn't enough.

There must also be what the Kerner Report calls by the old word "integration."

Now, I know that some people regard "integration" and "black power" as competing, antagonistic ideas. I guess I know that about as well as anybody does. And I know that some people regard "integration" as passé—an idea whose time has *passed*. (If so, it passed pretty fast. Now, in 1968, it is just four years since I sat in the Senate and listened to the closing argument by Senator Dirksen in which he announced dramatically that it was "an idea whose time has *come*.")

Well, I don't think integration and black power are competing ideas, nor do I think integration is passé. Instead I believe—as does the Kerner Commission—that we need "enrichment—plus integration." That means Neighborhood Strength—but also freedom to move out of the neighborhood. It also means fair employment practices, and open occupancy, and equal access to public accommodations and equal opportunity in public life, and desegregated schools.

So-called "integration" isn't enough, and it isn't the whole answer, but it is a necessity, a foundation, and a goal. It is where the modern movement for equality began; it remains *one* of its weapons in this fast-moving interim stage; it is what the movement will return to when the "interim" is over.

Maybe by then we will have found a better word for it. I certainly make no defense of the rather curious word "integration." I called it something else —"human rights"—on that hot afternoon in Philadelphia twenty years ago. "The bright sunshine of human rights" is pretty corny, but it got my meaning across at the time. "Human rights" or "equal opportunity" or whatever word you use remains and must remain a central American ideal and an abiding American purpose. We mean, by these phrases, an open access to the benefits of American life, without any barrier of color. That cannot be passé.

The first powerful "civil rights" or "integration" idea, in the modern period, was fair employment. Does any supporter of human rights seriously challenge that idea—that the law must insure equal opportunity in employment?

The most recent "integration" program is open occupancy. Nobody should erect racial barriers to the free choice of housing by any American. Nobody should tell anyone, on account of skin color, where he should and shouldn't live. Black power advocates can encourage blacks to stick together if they want to— but an individual Negro still should have a choice, and make his own decision, and not be blocked by racial barriers.

Leaders, Followers, Methods: Martin Luther King, Jr.

Who should lead us in new programs for participation? Who should follow? What methods should we use?

To answer that question I want to say a word about the greatest leader of the equal rights movement, Martin Luther King, Jr.

I remember that night of April 4, 1968, when I was waiting to address a Democratic Party dinner in a Washington hotel and a secret service man came up to me and said that Dr. King had been shot in a Memphis motel. Like millions of others around the world on that night I felt a sharp stab of shocked unbelief, of shame, and of grief. I broke the news to the large partisan crowd, which had just finished eating and was waiting for the evening program. They suddenly turned somber. We asked the House chaplain to say a prayer. After I sat down again I felt uncomfortable about going through with the evening's festivities. I spoke to the chairman, Senator Ed Muskie of Maine, and he quickly agreed that it wasn't right to go on with the partisan speechmaking. We called off the dinner and went home.

About all I said that night, under the first shock, was that this deed was "a shame upon our nation." I think it was. You can say that it was just one sick man who did the killing, but the violence, inequality, and racial prejudice in our country helped set the stage for it.

The murder of Dr. King did *not* mean that as a nation we had somehow lost our way. An assassin's bullet can no more indict an entire society in 1968 than it could in 1865 . . . or in 1963. But society's faults do contribute to the individual's deed.

We have our grave faults—but we also have, despite everything, our national virtues. You can emphasize the murder—or you can emphasize the life of Martin Luther King, Jr.

Dr. King's death snatched from American life something rare and precious: the living reminder that one man, by the force of his character, the depth of his convictions, and the eloquence of his voice, can alter the course of history.

Others knew Dr. King in the events of Montgomery and of Selma; I remember him most vividly in the great Washington March for Jobs and Freedom in August, 1963. That was a tremendous day. We had a good group from Minnesota, and I spoke to them early in the morning at an interracial church in Washington. The march as a whole turned out to be a huge throng—250,000 people. I remember the feeling as we walked together. It was like an immense town meeting —interracial, nation wide, ecumenical, one of the most beautiful occasions in American life. It was dissent with dignity, protest with decency, citizens peacefully petitioning their government. That day really started the immense coalition that led to the Civil Rights Act of 1964. And I think we should reconstitute that coalition.

It was late afternoon on that day at the Lincoln Memorial when Dr. King got up to talk—the last of the speakers.

"I have a dream," he said, "that on the red hills of Georgia the sons of former slaves and the sons of former slaveowners will be able to sit at the table of brotherhood . . .

"I have a dream that even the state of Mississippi, a state sweltering with the heat of injustice, will be transformed into an oasis of freedom . . .

"I have a dream—that my four little children will one day live in a nation where they will not be judged by the color of their skin but by the content of their character."

The crowd, rocking back and forth, would cry: "Dream some more."

Now his voice is silenced. But many of his own words are remembered as fitting interpretations of his life and his death. He said, for example: "If you are cut down in a movement which is designed to save the soul of a nation, then no other death could be more redemptive."

Most of us remembered, on that April night in 1968 when King was cut down, where we had been and how we had felt on November 22, 1963. I remembered also two other occasions in the violent history of our times when events made me weep. In June, 1963, after we had listened hopefully to President Kennedy's description of the civil rights bill, the newscast told of the cowardly murder of Medgar Evers, the leader of the NAACP in Mississippi. In September of the same year the news was even more horrifying: four children were killed while in Sunday School when a bomb exploded in their Birmingham church. Two months after the killing of Dr. King, there was to be yet another in this dreadful series of violent events, when Robert Kennedy was killed in Los Angeles.

Martin Luther King, Jr., was the greatest modern spokesman against such violence, and against the hatred that leads to such violence. But he was more than a leader of "non-violence."

I think some of the reaction to Dr. King's murder in the days that followed missed the point—and I do not mean just the looting, rioting, and burning.

Hundreds of commentators were quick to say that pillage, arson, and violence in the streets dishonored the man who died—and that was true. It was so obviously true that it scarcely needed to be said.

But there are also more subtle ways to distort the meaning of his life. Too much of the first white reaction to his death was that of fear rather than of grief and shame. Too often there was only anxiety about what would happen. Dr. King seemed to be thought of as a restrainer of Negroes, instead of a fighter for equality. Public comment often implied that he was solely a Negro leader for non-violence instead of a world leader for justice and peace.

Martin Luther King, Jr., was "an apostle of non-violence." But it is not enough to say that. He was an apostle of social justice by means of non-violent direct action. Social justice comes first.

To be non-violent while sitting on the sidelines is easy enough; to be non-violent in the midst of the fight is something else. It is not very significant if a man is non-violent while he is doing nothing. It is significant if a man is non-violent while he is risking his life to change society.

To combine passion for justice with the arduous

discipline of non-violence requires an unusual spirit. When we see that severe and difficult moral discipline embodied in a man, we are all better for it. It teaches us a lesson that we badly need. The lesson is—to fight hard for justice, without giving way to hate, without breaking the bonds of community, without destroying those whom we must oppose. The lesson is—we can act to change America's wrongs, while remaining ready for reconciliation with all of America's people. Put the other way around, the lesson is—to love and be non-violent, but to fight actively against social injustice all the same.

Dr. King fought for racial equality, for human dignity, for justice in society. He went back to Memphis not just to preach non-violence but to engage in a direct-action protest to help that city's garbage collectors and that city's poor.

It comes with poor grace from the comfortable people in our society to underline Martin Luther King's message when he says "non-violence" (if he says it to the Negroes and the poor), but then to be deaf when he says "justice" and "racial equality" to us.

And it is not right to remember him as a leader only of Negroes.

Too many white commentators keep asking: "Who will succeed Dr. King?" The implication of this question seems to be: Who will keep the Negroes non-violent? Who will teach them moderation? Who will keep the lid on the ghetto?

I can understand why Whitney Young, Jr., said that we ought to get over this notion of ethnic leaders,

"Negro" leaders, and talk instead about leaders for justice and decency—leaders of all colors. Whitney Young is one, Martin Luther King was one, Robert Kennedy was one. The issue is not between black leaders and white leaders, but between leaders for justice and decency and those who would take us in the other direction.

Sometimes it is said that Dr. King was a "leader of his people." But what does that phrase "his people" mean?

I am one of his people. You are one of his people. He was a leader of us all. He was a member of the human race, as you and I are; he honored us all.

He was an American, as you are I are; as such, he honored the country of which we are all equally citizens.

White people say, defensively, that they are not guilty of the murder of Dr. King; he was killed, they say, by one man, not by the whole white race. And that is true.

But if we reject the racial guilt in this case, we must also reject every idea of racial guilt in every other case—including the looting and arson and rioting of a very small fraction of Negroes (along with some whites).

And though we can reject the idea of racial guilt, we must accept the idea of social responsibility.

People who have power and privilege, people who can affect the shape of society, people who can bring justice and equality if they will—all such people, all of us, do have a responsibility both for the conditions that brought Dr. King to Memphis and the conditions that make for riots. So we all have to rejoin—or join for the first time—the coalition for social justice that is America at its best.

Dr. King lived and died to make men aware of their social responsibility. We will honor him not by fearing each other but by accepting together that responsibility to bring full racial equality and economic justice to his country.

8

Beyond Civil Rights:
The Continuing
American Revolution

The United States has had many inequalities and injustices: sectional favoritism and rivalry, to the disadvantage of the South and the West; class barriers, between the well-to-do and people from the wrong side of the tracks; "nativist" mistreatment of the immigrants who came to this country on a slightly later boat. We have also had religious and "ethnic" discrimination, often linked to the nativists' resistance to the immigrant. When my father campaigned in Doland for those five votes for Al Smith in 1928, the main thing he had to resist was anti-Catholicism. It was still evident even in 1960, when John Kennedy ran for President. It was a major consideration in the primaries between Kennedy and me, and markedly distorted the results of the presidential election that year between Kennedy and Nixon.

The worst of all prejudices and discriminations in the history of European civilization—anti-Semitism—has also been an ugly part of American history.

Many groups other than Negroes have suffered many injustices in this country. There are the Americans with Spanish surnames, in the Southwest and in the Puerto Rican sections of New York and other cities—five million people, the nation's second largest "minority."

These Spanish Americans, Mexican Americans, and Puerto Ricans have been badly treated. They feel that most of the reformers' efforts are directed to the Negro, and too little to them. One recent anthology on poverty lists in its index fifty-nine references to Negroes, only one to Spanish-surname Americans. Yet they face poverty, neglect, and prejudice, too. They have distinct problems of language; one school administrator in a Southwestern city remarked that the schools there had the distinction of graduating students who were functionally illiterate in two languages.

Our citizens and residents of Oriental background have been unfairly treated—not least by the terrible racial bias that long excluded them from American society. And one of the worst deeds the American nation ever committed was the Japanese "relocation" during World War II—racist in conception, a violation of our basic liberties, making the equivalent of concentration camps on our own soil.

The original American, the Indian, has been mistreated ever since the white man landed here. President Johnson's 1968 presidential message to Congress on the American Indian—the first such message in history —gave statistics about the condition of the 600,000 American Indians that were even more stark than those about the Negro: nearly forty percent are unemployed; 50,000 live in substandard dwellings; fifty percent of the children drop out of school; the average age of death of the Indian is forty-four years (for all other Americans, sixty-five). We have established a new Council of Indian Opportunity, of which I am chairman, to focus the full resources of many agencies of the federal government on the pressing and long-neglected economic and social problems of the Indian American— in some ways the worst treated of all minorities.

Many inequalities have nothing to do with color or with membership in a minority group. Although the proportion of Negroes who are poor, unemployed, and subject to mistreatment is much larger than that of whites, still the *total number* of whites is larger, just because the large majority in the nation is white. There are more white poor than black poor; there are more white unemployed, more white slum-dwellers, more whites on welfare than there are Negroes. It is understandable, perhaps, that some of the white poor and white ex-poor, who have had their own severe difficulties, do not fully comprehend why the problem of the Negro is much different from their own.

Irish Americans in South Boston, Italian Americans in Providence, Polish Americans in Buffalo, the child of immigrants from Central Europe who lives in Cleveland may feel the Negro is being favored. A common theme goes like this: "When my grandfather came over from the old country, nobody helped *him; he* didn't have any civil rights laws."

The white man in the hills and the hinterland who does not himself have any of that "affluence" or any of that participation in the "white power structure" that he hears so much about may be particularly resentful of what appears to him to be favoritism to the Negro. If he lives in the South he may feel the sting also of sweeping moralistic denunciations of his whole region.

Being the victim of mistreatment does not, however, justify anyone's participating in mistreating another.

That is true of the white man in the hills, and of the black man repeating anti-Semitic slogans on the city streets. Prejudice and hatred and racism are evils that cannot be defended.

We do need to be aware of the gamut of injustice and inequality that there can be in a complicated society— wide-ranging, changing, not always fitting the established categories of oppressed and oppressors. Individuals may have a very different place, in the pattern of social justice, from that assigned to them by stereotype. Things change. Yesterday's victims of injustice may become tomorrow's perpetrators of it.

Some legitimate grievances are overlooked in the standard slogans of the doctrinaire. Many of the white rural poor have been badly treated by social circumstance—and in some instances, overlooked by reformers. Many white working people, in a financial and social situation that is not too secure, feel themselves very much threatened and unjustly treated in the current atmosphere. They feel that nobody hears their cry, or cares about their situation, and that it is nevertheless they and not the reformers who have to bear the costs of today's rapid social change. Although you cannot accept as just all of their complaints and resentments (nor those of anybody else either, including the poor), still these people, too, deserve to be heard.

We all do. That is why our standard of judgment in the last analysis is not some group's power (black, white, brown, red, or blue blood) but an *equal* opportunity for *persons*.

Do you want a society that is nothing but an endless power struggle among organized groups? Do you want a society where there is no place for the independent individual? I don't. I don't think the American people do. The organized power of groups is and should be an important part of democratic politics—but it is not the whole story. Equal justice under law and equal opportunity for all persons to develop themselves—that is what we seek.

Sometimes I hear the phrase "human resources," and it makes me wince a little. I hear it said that young Americans in school are "the greatest resources we have"—which is entirely true, but not the most essential point. I hear it said that the racial abominations in our American history—slavery, segregation, discrimination, holding the Negro down—have resulted in a terrible waste of human resources to the nation: we have missed all the additional contributions that all the black children might have made if they had had full opportunity. And that's altogether true, too—but it is not the place to begin. The poor are spoken of in this way, too: as a neglected national resource, even sometimes as a great body of potential purchasers of commodities who ought to be brought into the consumer economy.

All of these points about the potential value of human beings to the society and to the economy are sound and true at their own level—but their level is not the highest one.

We seek full education for every child first of all because we affirm the worth of the child; we seek to overthrow the barriers of race not only to make our country stronger and richer—which it will—but because those barriers are unjust; we seek a society where human development comes first not only because our citizens are a "resource," like coal or oil, but because human development is what America is, or should be, all about—in Doland and in Harlem.

Many millions of individuals have been denied opportunity to develop themselves, and their lives have been stunted by our terrible national history of slavery, segregation, and discrimination. White Americans by and large still do not fully admit this—but it is true.

The United States had until the Civil War the worst example of human slavery in modern history.

The nation promised, after the war was over and freedom came, that it would grant to Negro citizens equality that should never have been denied them—but then it didn't deliver on that promise. On the contrary: the nation allowed the imposition of *new* inequalities and injustices.

Why did this happen? Because the American people —and the North in particular—failed to follow through realistically on the commitments they had made. Too much of the effort to deal with this American problem has been sectional: the North blaming the South, and the South being monolithically defensive. But the "North" has been heavily involved in the nation's problem, from the days of the Yankee slave traders to the racism in Northern cities today.

Many of the abolitionists and reformers were legalistic and emotional absolutists, who simply wanted slavery abolished—period. After the Civil War they turned to other causes or to private pursuits, forgetting the newly freed Negro. But emancipation should have been the beginning and not the end of their crusade.

The Negro—after being subjected to the cruel and crushing institution of slavery—prohibited by law, for example, from an education—needed a great deal more than abstract freedom. But though there were many philanthropic efforts by a small minority of whites, the North as a whole, and the federal government in particular, soon left the Negro to the control of segregationist whites.

There is a lesson in that for today, because we could do the same thing again. The distinguished Southern historian C. Vann Woodward made this observation:

> Americans have developed over the years a curious usage of the law as an appeasement of moralists and reformers. Given sufficient pressure for a law that embodies reputable and popular moral values, the electorate will go to great lengths to gratify the reformers . . . But having done this much, they are inclined to regard it as rather tedious of the reformers to insist on literal enforcement. Under these circumstances the new law is likely to become the subject of pious reference, more honored in the breach than in the observance, a proof of excellent intentions rather than the means of fulfilling them.

Professor Woodward, writing in 1957, added that that might happen again with the Supreme Court's school segregation decision. Now, eleven years later, we can say that it might happen again with the Civil Rights Act of 1964 and 1965 and 1968, and with all the other actions of this past decade and a half of civil rights action.

Once more we are in the tough second stage, the stage of the application and enforcement and follow-through, the stage of shaping new institutions rather than rous-

ing moral fervor, the stage of complexity rather than
simplicity. This is the time when we should stop casti-
gating others for past wrongs and turn to the common
task of building a humane future. We are once again
in the period when professional agitators tend to demand vengeance for racial wrongs and indulge in ex-
tremist rhetoric, and when the white public tends to become annoyed—or turns negative. This is the time that
most needs patient, practical, persistent work—and the
time when the public mood makes it most difficult to
carry on such work. This is the *hard* period, the time
of real testing.

Last time we as a nation failed the test.

It is not too much to say that all the hopes which mankind has had for this unusual and fortunate nation of
America depend upon what we now do—to make real
the American promise of equality to Negroes.

We have already accomplished a great deal. We have
turned this country around, from a situation in which
the nation's laws and governments *allowed* and even
required racial segregation and discrimination to one in
which laws and governments *oppose* and *attack* segregation and discrimination.

In this time of national self-doubt we need to see our
efforts to achieve equal rights in historical perspective,
and not to discount what America recently has done.
We started very late to correct this nation's one huge
wrong. We really just began to overturn the slave
culture with A. Philip Randolph's March on Washington and Franklin Roosevelt's Order 8802—little more
than a quarter of a century ago. And that was a limited
wartime measure. We brought civil rights into the

mainstream of American politics just two decades ago. The first giant step was taken fourteen years ago by the Supreme Court, and faced great resistance. The first large and successful demonstration came thirteen years ago. The first congressional action, eleven years ago; and spreading public participation just within this decade. We have done more for racial equality in the 1960's than in all the prior three-hundred-and-more-year history of the white man on this continent.

America's efforts also should be seen in a comparative context. We are one of the most heterogeneous nations in the world—even in the history of the world. Despite our heterogeneity and the cruel caste-slavery system we inherited, we have not had the blood bath between races and peoples that has marked the history of other heterogeneous nations, some of which sometimes look down in moral disdain upon the United States. Other countries, like England, that have rightly been critical of America's racial injustice discover now that they cannot prevent the stupid and cruel problems of color from arising in their own land.

No nation is free from the terrible burdens of historic evils; no nation is composed of angels, free from human frailty. The relevant question is not—is this people perfect? but—what are they doing about their imperfections? In what direction are they moving—and how fast?

It is a historic accomplishment to have swung American law and government around to the side of equality. That has happened in your lifetime and mine. Its full effect has still not been felt. It happened *against* the very strong resistance of many people's racism, inherited from the slave-segregation past. There isn't much doubt that the laws and court decisions go far beyond what the mass of the people, trapped in old fears and prejudices, would have endorsed.

The strength and flexibility of America's constitutional system made this possible. The breadth and rightness of America's ideals made this possible. America's institutions and ideals can now support a still greater accomplishment—making equality a reality in everyday life.

In America's past there is the terrible fact of slavery and discrimination. In America's present there is the disgrace of poverty and racial injustice. But those are not reasons to repudiate American institutions and American ideals. These institutions and ideals can prove once more their value as we progress toward full equality.

When you hear angry men denounce America, ask yourself these questions: What sort of a nation would it be if their ideals prevailed? What sort of national institutions would they build? Would their institutions permit orderly protest, progress, and change? Would they protect those who disagree with them? Would their ideals encourage human variety and toleration and—yes—brotherhood?

Let me use this analogy: negativism about America can be like negativism about a Negro child's ability to learn in school. If a bigoted teacher expects nothing from this Negro child, then her expectations will probably be fulfilled. It's a self-fulfilling expectation. In the same way, if the best of our young people, our idealists, our preachers, and prophets condemn and disdain the

American system, and expect nothing from it—then in the long run their expectations may prove true, because they have made it so.

Our American institutions need the healthy probing of continuing criticism—but criticism that is selective, specific, and informed. We need criticism that reflects particular objective evils, not a subjective mood of cynicism, self-indulgence, or complete estrangement.

The distinguished former Secretary of Health, Education and Welfare, John Gardner, has remarked that we seem to be dividing into unloving critics and uncritical lovers of American institutions. Obviously, what we need are critical lovers of America—patriots who express their faith in their country by working to *improve* it.

We seek to complete the unfinished peaceful American revolution, not to inaugurate a new and violent one —nor to sit comfortably where we are.

I said at the start of this book that we have been seeking and are seeking equality and reconciliation under the law: equality first of all, but in the context of reconciliation and of law.

Equality—or equal freedom for all—is the objective of the never-ending American revolution. Opponents of democracy have always made arguments against that goal. It really means human dignity. Human dignity requires pride and self-respect; self-respect depends in part on the respect of one's fellows. When groups of people are treated without respect, they undervalue themselves. The greatest evils of discrimination and poverty are not hunger and physical misery, bad as they are, but humiliation and spiritual misery; being treated as less than a man—unequally—without dignity.

The first stage in the unfinished American revolution toward human dignity was legislation for civil rights—the anti-discrimination laws postponed for a hundred years, but now at last enacted. They are the laws of the land: fair employment, fair housing, open public accommodation, no segregated schools. Government agencies are set up to enforce this law of equal opportunity and equal treatment.

But this is just a start. In the current stage we must deal with the *past* effects of racial injustice—men must be helped to lift themselves out of the sad country of poverty to which generation after generation of racial discrimination has consigned them.

The human rights movement and the Negro community today stand at the center of that continuing American revolution—the ongoing movement of critical lovers of America working toward a wider realization of American ideals.

The black American has lived in the midst of the land of the free, breathing the air of freedom, and yet has been only half-free himself. He has lived in a country whose founding document says that all men are created equal, and yet has been treated as a less-than-equal himself. As men escaping from a totalitarian country appreciate the meaning of freedom in a way that citizens of a free country often do not (they take it too much for granted), so in a more complex and ironic way the Negro knows American ideals. He has lived with them in their sincerity and in their hypocrisy.

He has lived much of the time in the Other America. He has lived for a century with one foot in American democracy. And now his day at last has come, when he enters full-fledged into American society. Out of all of his suffering he is teaching his country something, about her virtues and her faults, her ideals and her realities. America will be a far better country when it learns what he has to teach.

We hear more and more today about the Negro's contribution to America—in the arts and the sciences, in scholarship and sports, in entertainment and in war; we are even learning that there were Negro cowboys. This current recovery of the forgotten history of black America is good and necessary. But there is also a broader kind of "contribution" of the Negro to his America, too, alongside all the individual poets and preachers and leaders: the contribution of a whole people's faith—a people who kept faith with their country even when it did not keep its promises to them.

Let me turn once more to Ralph Ellison, again from the hearings before the Ribicoff committee:

> As far as responsibility goes, I hold my own group for instructing others in our view of American reality. I hold that it is necessary that we insist upon the importance of our own reality. Otherwise I must ignore the dynamics of some ninety years of history during which American white people have been disciplined to be as vaguely aware of the humanity of Negroes as possible.
>
> This is the reality, and I don't see how we can overcome it unless we approach it consciously. Society has been structured so that you will not know me and I will not know you, and to accept this gulf in understanding as part of my given American situation. And when we fail to do this, then we

Negroes fail our responsibility as citizens. Unfortunately, our leadership has been powerless for so long, simply because there was no legal basis upon which Negroes could be organized, that they could not give the larger American society a sense of the human complexity of this group of Americans which has grown up in this country under the condition of slavery, who survived various types of brutalization, and who is here today with much to offer the nation, because we have lived with the experience which is to be found among most colonial peoples. All of the dynamics of the future are right here among American Negroes, and we have the responsibility not to give you the cliché of sociology, but to tell you exactly what it is that we feel and how we view the world.

Negroes would like to be responsible for part of the life, the quality of life, in the United States, not just because we are a big legal reality, but because we are a conscious, responsible people who have the opportunity to express that little bit of wisdom which we have gained through our denials.

Mr. Ellison suggests the many contributions the black man can give American society today: deepening our national self-understanding and self-criticism; illuminating our understanding of the colonial peoples abroad and of the world's future; providing insight into human relations and into our own past. More practically, black Americans can provide the insight and the votes to bring a new progressive politics to the American city. And black Americans can help to do the same in the New South, and throughout the nation.

This "contribution" that these Americans are making and will make, is of great benefit to the nation as a whole. In much of what has been done in the civil rights movement, Negroes and whites have worked together.

And the impact has reached beyond civil rights and beyond the Negro community, with beneficial effects throughout American society. It led to a new concern for other disadvantaged groups: Spanish-surname Americans, Indians, the rural and urban poor. It is forcing a constructive examination of many American institutions—the public schools, for a most important example, and the welfare system and the police and the legal system and the housing industry. It posed new questions about city government and state government, about health care and family rehabilitation, about the social responsibility of business and labor. It helped to revive social idealism in the American people, in the churches and the universities, and especially among the young.

In the fifties much public discussion dealt with the dangers of conformity of the organization man in his gray flannel suit and his split-level house; discussion about schools centered on why a rather middle-class Johnny couldn't read; discussion about a passive college generation referred to them as "young fogies"; many citizens complacently assumed we had no serious domestic problems, only international ones.

There were many reasons for the change in the nation's spirit between the mid-fifties and the mid-sixties —but the most important single reason was the great civic coalition that we called the civil rights movement. It helped to revive a sense of public purpose in America. It renewed the humane spirit of American social idealism, and aroused that spirit in a new generation. We must reconstitute that great coalition.

The struggle for equal opportunity in America is the

struggle for America's soul. The ugliness of bigotry stands in direct contradiction to the very meaning of America.

Langston Hughes wrote a poem called "Let America Be American Again" which expresses the idea that ours is an uncompleted nation, a country that has not yet become what it is truly supposed to be. His lines refer repeatedly to the hopes for America of Americans of many kinds and conditions, and concludes: "We the people must redeem our land. . . and make America again!" One stanza summarizes what I have been trying to say:

> Oh, let America be America again,
> The land that never has been yet.
>   and yet must be—
> The land where every man is free.